Return to Palm Court

Stephanie Edwards

About Brittany Nelson, the main character

Q: Why did you choose to write Brittany as deaf?
A: I've always wanted to write a book about a woman who leads an ordinary life, but also is deaf. Brittany has a fiancé, graduated from college and wants the same things out of life that most young women want.

Q: Why was this important to you?
A: Several family members and other people who made a strong impression on me during my childhood are deaf. I've watched them live mostly normal lives. I wanted to share the lessons I've learned from them with others. Also, I've always loved seeing the success stories of anyone who squashes obstacles they face, whether that's a communication-related need, a learning disability or a mental health challenge.

Q: How can I tell if Brittany is signing or speaking orally in the book?
A: It becomes redundant to say, "she signed" or "stepped back to read his lips," but I made a note of it where I felt it added significance to the scene. In the places where I don't specify a communication method, the reader can assume that if Brittany is with her family, she is signing, or if she's with other people or spirits, she is speaking.

Q: What do you hope readers take away with them after reading about a deaf character?
A: I want them to understand that being deaf hasn't held Brittany back. She can read lips and speak orally and through American Sign Language (ASL). She went through an extensive early intervention program that helped her learn how to do these things. Also, the interventionist helped her family learn how to sign and support her in life. Every deaf person's journey and how they communicate is different. Brittany's story is just one representation.

To my deaf family members and friends – thank you for always accepting me. I love you!

Susan

1996

Prologue

S usan Nelson sat in the rocking chair beside the bed of her youngest daughter, Brittany, and watched the first rays of the morning sun peek through the blinds. She rubbed tired eyes before mopping Brittany's forehead with a cool cloth, giving silent thanks for the piping hot coffee she sipped in the moments not spent taking care of the sick toddler.

The poor girl had been sick with a fever, cough and runny nose for the past week. Her older sisters had skated by with just the sniffles.

Susan's husband entered the room, carrying a tray loaded with medicine, lime gelatin and toast. Jeremy set the tray on Brittany's dresser and measured out a dose of children's strength, pain and fever-reducing medicine. "Open up. It's time for your medicine."

The child didn't stir. Susan shrugged. "She must be exhausted, too. I'll try to wake her." She picked up Brittany, and the girl's blue eyes opened. "Good morning, beautiful. How are you feeling?"

Brittany rubbed her ears but didn't respond. Jeremy walked over to her, placing the measuring cup in her mouth. "Drink up, baby. Are you okay?"

1

"What did you say, Daddy? My ears are ouchie!"

Susan frowned. "Honey, Daddy and I both asked how you're feeling." As Susan put her back in bed, the child blinked and settled down without saying a word, not the norm for this rambunctious toddler.

"When did you take her temperature last?" Jeremy asked.

"About two hours ago. It was a low-grade fever—99.3—not too high. I'll recheck it, though." Brittany scrunched up her nose when Susan placed the thermometer under her tongue. After it beeped, Susan examined the result window. "Oh, gosh. It's climbing again, 100.5. We'll give the medicine a chance to work, but if it doesn't, we'll take her to the doctor."

Jeremy placed the food tray on the bed and handed Brittany a spoon to eat her gelatin. She took a couple of bites but threw the spoon onto the tray.

"Do you want a piece of toast?" he asked.

Brittany wrapped herself in her blanket and began trembling, shaking the entire bed.

Susan picked up the child and caressed her. "Jeremy, she is burning up and clammy. She needs to see a doctor right now. Call the pediatrician and ask if we should take her to his office or the ER."

He left the room and came back a few minutes later. "The doctor said he'll meet us at the hospital. His daughter lost her hearing due to a high fever when she was the same age as Brittany."

"Oh, God! Did he think that's what is happening to her?"

Jeremy grimaced. "He didn't say, but he wants us to bring her right now."

Susan sprang into motion, putting Brittany's socks, shoes and coat on her. "Let me grab a bottle of water and her medicine, and I'll take her."

"I'll go, too. I called my mom. She's on her way to watch Elaina and Blake."

Questions began racing through Susan's mind. What was happening to Brittany? What if she'd lost her hearing? If so, what would her life look like? How would she communicate? Would she succeed in school, in her career and romantic relationships? *Whatever the test results, I'll fight for my child and help her find her place in life regardless of any abilities she may or may not have. I won't let anything stand in her way of achieving her dreams.*

The front door opening interrupted Susan's thoughts. Her mother-in-law, Cora, must have arrived. She'd been a Godsend, especially considering that Susan's mother lived six hours away in South Carolina. Sure enough, Cora announced herself. "Grandma's here! Girls, come give me a hug!"

Footsteps thundered down the steps and across the kitchen floor to the living room. A chorus — "Yay! Grandma!" — echoed back to Brittany's first-floor bedroom.

Moments later, Cora joined them in Brittany's room. "What's the matter with my little Britt? Are you okay, baby?" Brittany lay facing the wall, holding her favorite baby doll. Cora locked eyes with Susan. "Goodness, that isn't like Brittany."

Tears threatened to stream down Susan's face, but she forced them back down. "We're going to get her checked out now. Thanks for watching the girls."

"Of course, dear. I hope everything's okay. Call me if you need anything."

"Thanks. We'll see you soon." Jeremy picked Brittany up and carried her to the car, Susan close behind.

No one talked during the 10-minute ride to the hospital. Susan looked over her shoulder to see Brittany asleep in her car seat. She prayed for a miracle for the innocent little girl and for God to protect her from a potentially life-altering loss.

As Jeremy pulled up to the entrance, Susan gathered her purse and coat. Her hands shaking, she jumped out of the car and fumbled with the buckle on Brittany's car seat. Picking up Brittany somehow comforted Susan. While Jeremy parked the car, she rushed the child into the ER admissions.

"Excuse me, Mrs. Nelson?"

She turned around to see Brittany's pediatrician, Dr. Matthews. "This little one is having a hard time."

"I'm so sorry to hear that. If you'll follow me, I've set up an examination room."

Jeremy joined them, and Susan let out a sigh of relief. "Thank you so much. We're beside ourselves."

A nurse began taking Brittany's vitals. "Dr. Matthews, her temp is 104.2." She turned to Susan. "What time was her last dose of medicine?"

"An hour ago." Susan frowned. "What can you do to help lower her temperature? Is she going to be okay?"

Dr. Matthews pursed his lips. "The nurses are going to get her an IV with some stronger medicine and to keep her hydrated. While they're working on that, have you heard of Cytomegalovirus?"

"No. What is that? Is that how your daughter…" Jeremy winced.

"It is rare but not unheard of for children to develop hearing loss or become deaf because of the virus. That being said, my daughter is one of them. I'm not saying Brittany has experienced permanent hearing loss, but when we're able to break the fever, we'll run some tests."

"Do whatever you need to do to help our baby."

"Of course, we'll do what we can. I'll be back to check on her shortly."

Susan stared at Brittany, curled up in the hospital bed, fast asleep. Jeremy sat on the corner of the mattress, holding the child's hand. They needed a miracle.

Wiping away a tear, Susan pulled out her long-distance calling card and provided her mother's phone number. Julia Caroline Mason may not be an angel, but she was the next best thing. When she heard her mother pick up the phone, she sighed. "Hi, Mom. Brittany's in the hospital—"

"Oh, dear! What is the matter?"

Susan gulped and explained what they knew so far. "Mom, what if she ends up losing her hearing? I'm not sure how to help her."

"Hon, we'll make everything work, no matter what. Try not to worry. I'll activate the prayer chain—you can never have too many people praying for you."

"You're right. Thanks for talking me through this. I have faith that it will work out in the end. I hate that I can't take on Brittany's burden for her, but I know she has all of us on her side to support her."

As Susan hung up the phone, the doctor returned. "Mrs. Nelson, the nurses told me Brittany's fever has broken, which is excellent news. We're going to take her to audiology for a hearing test. I'll bring her right back afterward and let you know the results."

After they'd left the room, Susan closed her eyes and slipped into a dreamless sleep.

Susan woke to the sound of the doctor pushing Brittany into the room on a child-sized gurney. She pulled herself upright in the recliner and smoothed her blouse. "How did the tests go?"

"Her hearing loss is worse than I thought. The good news is that Brittany had already learned how to speak, and she's very articulate for a toddler. If you get her hearing aids now and sign her up for Tennessee's state-wide early intervention program, she'll have a great chance of maintaining strong oral speech skills and learn how to read lips. The interventionist will help your family learn sign language, too. Brittany will have several options for communicating. I was lucky to be a doctor when my daughter got sick; otherwise, I might not have known who to turn to when our family needed help. I hope that this information helps Brittany and the rest of your family." He handed her a notecard with several resource phone numbers handwritten across the top.

Jeremy thanked him for his help, and Susan walked over to Brittany. Stroking the tot's hair, she took a deep breath. There was no question they'd face challenges on this journey, but she was determined to fight every obstacle alongside Brittany.

Chapter 1

B rittany Nelson imagined the roaring applause as she
looked out into the sea of people attending her
graduation ceremony. Was the sound of the large
crowd unnerving? She'd lost her hearing as a toddler. Her
late grandmother's singing had been etched in her mind, but
no matter how hard she tried, she couldn't remember hearing
anyone else's voice.

She wiped her sweaty palms on her gown and smiled at
her family. Granny Mason waved from the back of the arena.
Family matriarch Julia Caroline Mason was nearly 20 years
in her grave, but that didn't stop her from supporting her
granddaughters. Brittany waved back, gulping when she saw
a stranger talking to Julia. Who was this cheerful co-ed who
conversed with the dead? Brittany hadn't seen the young
blond woman around campus, but Atlanta University was a
huge school. The dean tapped her on the shoulder, and she
read his lips. "Brittany, smile for the photo. We've gotta keep
this line moving." Camera flashes stung her eyes, but she
complied. Shaking his hand, she posed for a photo and exited
the stage.

When she looked back, Granny Mason and her friend had
disappeared. The rest of her family stood, applauding and
signing, "Way to go," in American Sign Language. She
thanked them as she kept looking for the girl, but she had
disappeared.

Not sure if she'd imagined the whole thing, she tried to

brush it off and took her seat with her classmates. These strait-laced soon-to-be engineers, stockbrokers and teachers were in full party mode. But Brittany's thoughts distracted her from celebrating. She kept turning her head back to where her grandmother had been. Her sister, Blake, caught her eye and asked her what was wrong.

"Who was the girl talking to Granny Mason?" Brittany asked.

"Who? Where? I didn't see Granny."

"They were sitting right in front of you guys."

Their grandmother had explained that spirits could hide from each other and clairvoyant people. Maybe Granny Mason didn't want to be questioned about her newfound friend.

Blake turned, and Brittany saw her gaze zero in on something in the distance. She strained to see what had captured her sister's attention—Granny Mason and the woman sat five sections away, across the arena.

Brittany watched, puzzled, trying to determine this girl's identity. It was impossible from her vantage point. She needed to get closer, but the ceremony was still going full swing.

She got her sister's attention and signed, "Who is that?"

"I have no idea," Blake signed. "She looks familiar, but I can't put my finger on where I know her from."

"Can you get closer?"

Blake stood up and walked toward the women. Brittany watched as Blake smiled, shook the woman's hand and walked back to her seat. She looked at Brittany and signed, "That woman has spoken to spirits most of her life, and Granny's helping her figure out how to send an evil one on its way."

That sounded like her grandmother. "What's her name?"

Blake scrunched her face. "I forgot to ask."

"Really?" Brittany laughed. "You've always got your head up in the clouds."

"Yeah—just wait until you have kids. You'll see how little sleep you get. It messes with your brain."

There were circles under Blake's eyes, and her skin was more ashen than before she had become a mom.

I should offer to help with my niece more often.

Looking up, Brittany noticed the last row of graduates were in formation, waiting to cross the stage. Soon everyone took their seats again. The band's music vibrated and reverberated through her body as the university president walked up to the microphone. A sign language interpreter began translating, "Thank you to everyone who has offered their support to our graduates through their respective master's programs. Now, it's my pleasure to introduce the Class of 2021!"

A whoosh of air flooded the coliseum stage as the graduates jumped to their feet and threw their caps toward the ceiling. Grad school was over!

A group of Brittany's friends asked her to pose for some photos. After a dozen selfies, her family made their way down the steps. Before they made it to her, someone tapped her on the shoulder.

Brittany spun around to see Ryan, her fiancé, holding a bouquet of sunflowers. "How did you get away? You're so close to finishing your residency. Are you sure you should be here?"

Ryan laughed. "Geez. If I didn't know better, I'd think you didn't want me here. It's a pretty damn big deal that you just graduated with your master's degree in architecture."

Her cheeks flushed, and she kissed him. "I'm sorry. I'm just surprised. Why didn't you sit with my parents?"

He shrugged. "My flight arrived late, so I grabbed a seat near the entrance."

Before she could respond, her dad slapped her on the back, "Way to go, Britt!"

"Now, we need to grab some pictures, too!" her mom said, teary-eyed. "This is our last graduation until Macy graduates from kindergarten."

They grouped for a few shots until her dad protested, saying they had taken enough photos. "Let's go get some grub." Jeremy Nelson was always hungry. He patted his belly and grinned at Brittany, whose mouth was gaping.

"Dad, that was so embarrassing!" She rolled her eyes. "Thank God I'm done with school and won't see these people ever again."

Ryan grabbed her hand and kissed it. "I'm feeling a little weird right now, probably just jet lag. You guys go on and grab lunch. I'm going to go back to your apartment and wait for you."

Brittany locked eyes with him. "Are you sure you're okay? Do you want to have dinner delivered to my apartment instead?"

He flashed her a smile. "Nope. I'm just tired. I don't want to ruin your graduation dinner with your family. I'll be there waiting for you when you get back." He arched his eyebrow and winked.

Heat radiated from her chin and chest. "Hmm. Sounds like a plan." She gathered up her belongings and followed her family out to the car.

During the ride to the restaurant, she took in the Midtown Atlanta scenery. She was going to miss walking at Piedmont Park and shopping at Atlantic Station. Finally, they arrived at Mary Mac Tea Room, a comfort food haven, where the sweet tea flowed like water, and plates covered with fried chicken and okra were worth their weight in gold. Indulging in comfort food was worth the calories. The women in their family could pack on pounds quickly, but one meal wouldn't derail her healthy lifestyle. *Calories don't count today!* She'd just take a long walk the next day.

During lunch, her mom turned to her, "So what's the plan now that you've got your degree?"

Good question. What should Brittany do now? Ryan hadn't committed to either of the lucrative job offers he had waiting for him. She didn't want to begin her career just to

10

quit after he returned. Sure, she could start a job wherever she wanted and ask him to be happy living there, but that wasn't the foundation for a healthy marriage. They needed to decide where to live together. That was important to her. Besides, he was supposed to be back by September.

"Brittany...hello—uh, Mom asked you a question." Blake stared at her.

Brittany shrugged. "I don't know the answer. With Ryan's career still up in the air, I'm not ready to put down roots in any city. But I need to make some money so I can afford to live."

Blake's eyes widened, and she slapped the table. "Ohmygod! I've got the perfect idea. Do you wanna hear it?"

"Um..." Her sister could be impulsive. She had outgrown it somewhat since marrying Clint, but she still had her moments. Brittany cringed. "What's your suggestion?"

"Don't make that face! My ideas aren't that crazy, are they? Wait, don't answer that!" Blake giggled. "Why don't you work at the Mason B&B until Ryan comes home? I need all the help I can get, especially with Macy going through the excruciatingly terrible threes."

Brittany laughed. "You're forgetting a couple of details. I don't have the first clue about running a bed and breakfast or raising a kid."

"Neither did I a few years ago," Blake said. "And I can teach you what I know about both."

"True. Well, it would give us a chance to catch up before I move across the country."

Their mom signed the word for "sad" and pretended to cry. "Please don't go too far away."

"Mom, don't worry. Wherever we live, we'll visit a lot."

"I hope so. I want to see all of my grandbabies." She winked. "Macy needs cousins."

Brittany scowled and crossed her arms over her chest. "Really, Mom, already?" *We're not even married yet, and the baby talk has already started. Couldn't she give us at least a year before hounding us?* Brittany was in no hurry to start a family and wasn't sure if she ever wanted one.

Maybe it was selfish, but she wanted to enjoy her career and marriage before considering having children. She knew Ryan wanted to wait to have kids, too. Trips to surf in California, eat pasta in Italy and dive in Turks and Caicos were all on their bucket list.

"I promise, you guys will be the first to know when and if we decide to give up our freedom, but we have a lot of plans that don't involve little ones."

Blake laughed. "I remember this pressure all too well. Speaking of which, I miss my little monster, even though she's been a bit of a nightmare lately. Clint will be relieved when I get back tomorrow. It would be even easier if we had another set of hands. We'd be thrilled if you came to stay with us. Please say you'll do it."

Brittany grinned. "Let me talk to Ryan, just to make sure he's not expecting me to go to Seattle for the summer. Hanging out with you guys sounds like fun. Plus, in between the madness, I could work on my tan."

"I promise that we'll make time for fun, and we'll eat all the delicious Lowcountry food we can handle."

"You'd better! And, tempting me with shrimp and grits is pretty low." Brittany punched her sister on the shoulder. "I'll talk to Ryan tonight."

Chapter 2

After dinner, Brittany's parents dropped her off at her apartment. As they said their goodbyes, she took in the classic Tudor-style house, which she'd shared with the same three girls since their sophomore year of undergrad. They'd developed a strong sisterhood over the past five years, building bonds with each other's boyfriends, friends and families. *Crap! Leaving them tomorrow is going to be tough.* She'd expected to find Ryan in the middle of a video game with her best friend Sara's boyfriend, Joe. But when she opened the living room door, Sara and Joe were laser-focused on the TV, gripping game controllers in their hands. They didn't so much as acknowledge her presence as she walked past them.

Opening the door to her suite, Ryan wasn't on the bed or her couch. There was no sign of him in her study nook either. She walked to the bathroom where the mirror had fogged. She smiled at the thoughts of joining Ryan in the shower and called out, "Babe, I'm back. Good news—my family went back to the hotel so we're finally alone."

Although she preferred signing in American Sign Language, she often spoke with her voice and read lips, giving her the option to sign with her family and speak to friends and other people who didn't sign. Brittany was grateful her mother had insisted, from an early age, that she become proficient in both methods of communication.

She pulled off her black dress, lacy bra and panties, and

twisted her long, dark, wavy locks into a bun before opening the shower door. "Hey, scoot over. I'm joining you."

Ryan made room for her, kissing her neck and shoulders. "I've missed you. I've been dying to devour you all day."

"Agh! Same. I can't wait to live in the same city as you again. There are so many things I've been looking forward to…"

He flashed a sexy smile. Two blue eyes sparkled like ocean waves calling her to sea. As Brittany lost herself in their tide; her heart pounded; and desire overcame her. She ran her hand over his arms, letting her body meld with his and savoring every delicate touch and kiss until she'd had all she could take. Stepping out of the shower, he offered her a hand and helped her dry her skin before picking her up and carrying her to the bed, where they made love most of the night, stopping only to recharge and rehydrate.

Ryan pulled her in to cuddle and signed, "You're so beautiful. Hey, I've been wondering—when do you want to get married?"

Brittany sat up and hugged her knees. "I'm ready whenever you are. I'd figured we would wait until after your residency wrapped up at the end of the summer. Speaking of this summer, Blake asked me to move in with her and Clint for a few months. They need some help with Macy and the B&B. Since you're so busy with work, I figured it would be okay, but if you have other plans for us, I can always just go for a short visit instead."

"Definitely, babe. You deserve to have fun this summer. I know you'll be working, too, but try to enjoy this time before starting your career. I'm just now getting used to the grind." She leaned into his body, looping her arm through his. Brittany's eyelids began drooping.

Ryan sat up so she could see him sign, "Ugh. I can't believe I have to leave you again in the morning." Running his fingertips along her face, he continued, "I'll try not to wake you up when I leave. I love you." He kissed her forehead and cuddled up against her shoulder. In a matter of minutes, he'd fallen asleep and begun drooling on his pillow. Brittany giggled but wrapped her free arm around him. The sweetness of the moment comforted her, and she dozed off, dreaming of living the beach life on Isle of Palms.

The next day, Brittany packed her belongings into her SUV and said goodbye to her roommates. Leaving Atlanta was bittersweet. There were so many good memories there. But it was time to move on to the next stage in her life. She was looking forward to spending quality time with Blake's family before she and Ryan settled into their careers and married life. Macy was at a fun age. The tot loved playing with dolls, games and running around the yard or beach with Blake's dog, Willow. Even though Brittany wasn't sure if she wanted to be a mom, she loved her niece as if she were her own child. Being an aunt was enough—all the fun parts of being a mom without the responsibility.

Before she started her drive to South Carolina, she checked her social media feeds. Her favorite home and garden television show hosts had posted about restoring old homes, some supposedly haunted. They joked about the creepy events homeowners had reported to them, but Brittany knew the truth. Ghosts were just as real as people. For better or worse, she and her sisters had inherited the family gift for seeing and communicating with spirits. Five years ago, the spirit of Blake's former fiancé, Parker, had tormented the family at the Mason homestead. Recalling the tumultuous experience, Brittany shivered, but she took comfort in knowing they had sent Parker on to his next destination. *Thank God for that.*

In Parker's case, their family gift had been a curse. But the Nelson sisters were grateful for every moment they'd spent with their granny's loving spirit. Thanks to her wisdom and guidance, they banished the malevolent spirit. Brittany shuddered, shaking off the frightening memory. Hopefully, they wouldn't need to use that part of their gift again.

Thanks to the trip down memory lane, the four-and-a-half-hour drive seemed to fly by. Approaching the Isle of Palms Connector bridge, the salty ocean air filled the car; the sunlight glistened on the green spartina grass, giving it a buttery glow. *Almost there.* When she pulled into the cottage driveway, she gasped. Blake and Clint had breathed new life into their family home. Gone were the crackled paint and weathered shutters, and in their place was an elegant exterior—a fine Southern lady ready to receive guests.

The front door flew open to reveal Blake, smiling ear to ear and holding out her arms to embrace Brittany and lead her into the house. "Macy has been talking up a storm about you ever since I got home this morning. Wait until she sees you. She's gonna freak out!"

Brittany peered over her sister's shoulder, but there was no sign of the child. "Where *is* Macy?"

Her three-year-old niece hopped into the living room from the kitchen. The child's dark ringlets bounced in time with her feet, and a thick, white milk mustache painted the top of her smile. "Auntie Britt, you're here," her tiny hands signed. "I love you!"

"Hey, cutie!" Brittany ruffled her hair and pulled her in for a hug.

"I colored a picture for you." Macy handed Brittany a folded piece of paper. Brittany opened it to look at her niece's artwork to see three stick figures. She grinned, folded the paper and put it into her pocket.

"It's me, you and my friend." Macy sipped milk out of her cup. "Friends are fun!"

"Thanks, Macy! I love it."

The child's green eyes shimmered in the bright room, and she spun around in a circle.

Blake smiled. "Honey, can you go play in your room while Aunt Britt and I unpack her car?"

"Yep, yep." The toddler nodded and walked upstairs.

For the next hour, Brittany and Blake unloaded the car with the intense South Carolina sun beating down on them. Brittany wiped her glistening forehead with her hand. "Hey, sis, I need a break."

Blake nodded. "Sounds good. I packed the fridge full of drinks. It's not even officially summer yet, but it's already hotter than blue blazes." They walked into the kitchen, and each poured a glass of sweet tea, the nectar of the gods. Brittany emptied the glass in a few big gulps.

"So, how's Ryan getting along in Seattle?" Blake asked, refilling their glasses and topping them off with some orange slices from the refrigerator.

"He seems happy. You know how modest he is. I'm sure he's the star resident. They've already offered to extend his contract. I'd rather not think about that, though." Brittany fidgeted with the zipper on her hoodie.

"It's gotta be hard not knowing when he will be home, especially when you're trying to figure out what you want out of life, too. I'm so proud of you for being so supportive of him. You guys are going to have an awesome life together."

Brittany sighed. "Well, he'd do the same for me." Ready to change the subject, Brittany stood. "I guess I'd better get back to unloading the car."

They walked outside and grabbed two boxes of clothing. Brittany shifted the heavy box in her hands, trying to get a better grip as they walked into the cottage.

A boom shook the house, and Brittany cowered, looking at the ceiling before glancing at her sister. "What happened?"

"I don't know." Blake's eyes widened and shifted toward the staircase. "Macy is screaming!"

Blake and Brittany dropped the boxes without missing a beat and ran up the steps to Macy's room. Brittany's heart in her throat, she focused on steadying her breathing. *Being a mom must be hard. Was she wired to handle emergencies, break fevers and clean up kid puke? What if her kid got hurt and screamed? She couldn't hear them; what if she didn't respond quickly enough?*

Blake made it into the room first. Brittany watched her sister's jaw drop as she screamed, "Oh, no!"

Before Brittany could bring herself to look, she mumbled a quick prayer for her niece's safety. Nothing could have prepared her for seeing a red-faced, sobbing Macy lying on the floor surrounded by shards of glass from the window. The panes had shattered inward as if someone or something had broken it from the outside. But how? There wasn't a ladder, a tree or even latticework nearby. No human could have climbed that high without a miracle, or at least a jet pack. In the blink of an eye, Blake lunged across the room and picked up the frightened child, careful to avoid the broken glass.

Shaking, she examined her for any obvious injuries and turned to Brittany. "Do you see any major cuts or bruises?"

"No—thank goodness!" Brittany clutched her heart. "I don't know how, but she only has a few small cuts and scratches on her arms and feet."

Tears filled Blake's eyes as she cradled Macy. Brittany had never seen her sister quite so upset. Blake rocked Macy for several minutes. When she calmed, she loosened her embrace and looked Macy in the eyes.

"What happened, honey? How did the window break?"

Macy's lip quivered. "Mama, my friend pushed me."

"Your friend? No one's here except Aunt Brittany and me."

"My friend is here." Macy pointed to the window. "He wanted me to go outside and play with him."

A chill crept down Brittany's back. Everyone had imaginary friends at this age. Didn't they? Maybe she was afraid of getting into trouble and had made up a story. She looked at her sister, who shrugged.

"She keeps scaring me to death. Last week, she locked herself in her closet. She always blames her imaginary friend," Blake signed.

"Do you think it's an imaginary friend, or could it be…"

Blake shook her head. "I haven't seen anyone. She has an overactive imagination. I'm terrified that she is going to hurt herself."

Brittany shuddered and ran to the hall closet to retrieve a broom and dustpan.

After cleaning up, Blake picked up Macy. "I think I'll run her over to the pediatrician's office just for a quick check-up to make sure she's 100 percent okay."

"That's a good idea. Better safe than sorry," Brittany said.

Macy wrapped her arms and legs around Blake's upper torso and sucked her thumb. "But I wanna stay and play with Auntie Britt. No ouchies! Me okay!"

Brittany kissed Macy's forehead. "Good luck at the doctor's office. Be good and do whatever your mom asks you to do, okay?" She paused for a moment, and Macy nodded. "If you're good at the doctor's office, and I mean a perfect angel, I'll make you one of my famous root beer floats."

"With chocolate ice cream and sprinkles?"

"Whatever you want, kiddo." Brittany ruffled the child's hair as Blake carried Macy out of the room.

She breathed a sigh of relief, grateful for Macy's clean bill of health and that she wasn't the one ultimately responsible for that innocent little life.

Chapter 3

B rittany picked up the boxes she and Blake had dropped and carried them up to her room. Sorting through her belongings, she found a framed picture of her and Ryan at homecoming. She hugged the photo to her chest and placed it on her nightstand. *I love that man!* She needed to talk to Ryan, but it was the middle of his workday. A full conversation would have to wait, so she sent him a quick text to let him know she was getting settled on the island.

The room grew darker, and a chill tingled down Brittany's spine. She looked at her smartwatch. Blake had left for the hospital more than three hours ago. *Hopefully, Macy's doctor visit went okay.* A thud from downstairs shook the floor under her feet. She pushed her phone into her pocket and ran, taking two steps at a time. Inhaling, she caught her breath in time to see the kitchen door was open. She grabbed a knife from the block on the countertop and scanned the living room to see if her sister had returned, but no one was there.

Vibration from footsteps filtered into the kitchen. Brittany followed the rhythmic steps, looking out the window to see a man picking pink roses from her granny's garden. Flinging the heavy oak and screen doors open, she stomped, ready to give him an earful.

The man turned in one swift motion, and Brittany let out a pained cry. *It couldn't be. It's not possible.* Their granny had been certain the deranged spirit of Blake's ex, Parker, had gone to his final resting place, yet here he was in the flesh, well, not the *flesh,* but, at any rate, it was him.

"Why in the hell are you here?" Brittany demanded, slamming her hands down onto a nearby table.

Parker's mouth twisted into an evil smile. "Now, is that any way to greet a long-lost friend? I was so good to you and your sister. You just never gave me a chance to prove just how *good* I am." He threw his head back, laughing, and vanished into a silvery mist. Was this a onetime respite from his new home, or had he returned to torment their family? Brittany couldn't stop her breakfast from coming up and hurled into the rose bushes, her knees buckling. Sweat beaded on Brittany's brow, and she sat down on the grass and cried.

There was no way she could tell Blake. Parker's return would frighten her sister. Brittany would keep this from her as long as possible. Lying to her would be hard. They'd always been close and told each other everything. When the spirit had unleashed chaos in their lives during his first haunting, Brittany and their sister, Elaina, had stepped up to help Blake banish him to his supposed final resting place. *Oh, Parker, why couldn't you have stayed put?*

Brittany needed to pull herself together. Blake and Macy couldn't see her like this. She ran to the downstairs powder room to wash her face. When Brittany came out, Blake's husband, Clint, was sitting at the kitchen table. He didn't sign, so she tried to clear the lump in her throat.

She forced a smile. "Have you heard from Blake?"

"Hey, yeah. I met Blake and Macy at the hospital. They're getting to know us on a first-name basis there. That kid is so accident prone." Clint shook his head.

"But she's okay?" Brittany asked. "What is going on with her?"

"It's a miracle, but she has these scary incidents every other week. Fortunately, she comes away without so much as a bump or bruise."

21

Brittany nodded and patted him on the shoulder. Clint was a good husband and father. She was glad Blake had married him. If she had married Parker, her life would be quite different. Brittany certainly wouldn't have moved to South Carolina for the summer. Now, the dead jerk had dared to return in his spiritual form. *Again, how was it even possible? Where was Granny Mason?*

"There's something I need to tell you, but you have to promise not to tell Blake." She bit her lip. This wouldn't go over well. Clint and Blake were as thick as thieves and never kept secrets from each other. Clint tilted his head and narrowed his eyes.

"I just saw Parker." Brittany cringed, wringing her hands.

Clint smiled as if he were waiting for the punchline of a joke. "That's not funny, Britt."

"I'm totally serious." Brittany stared at him.

His jaw dropped. "What? No. There has to be another explanation."

"Nope. We exchanged words."

"Damn it! I thought we took care of him before the wedding. How did he get back here?"

Brittany shrugged. "I have no idea, but this is terrible news. I don't want Blake to find out. I'll try to banish him on my own."

Clint gulped but didn't say a word.

"You won't tell Blake, will you?" Brittany arched her eyebrows. This one time, she needed him to make an exception to their honesty policy. It would only hurt her sister to know that her paranormal stalker had returned.

He rubbed his temples. "No. You're right. If you can make this go away like it never happened, that would be best for her…for all of us."

Brittany drew a deep breath and exhaled. Thank goodness Clint trusted her. Hopefully, she'd be able to chat with Granny Mason before Blake noticed anything out of the ordinary. Speaking of her sister, Blake and Macy should be home any minute. She took the remaining boxes upstairs and changed her outfit before returning to the kitchen.

Macy burst through the door. Her little hands flew through the air. "Auntie Britt! The doctor said I'm a good girl, no boo-boos. He gave me a sticker and a sucker!"

"Awesome, girl! I'm so glad. Let's go get your root beer float!" Brittany grabbed her niece's hand and walked into the kitchen. *Thank goodness she's okay!* Everyone in the family loved her. Brittany had done her part in spoiling Macy. One thing's for sure; their mom hadn't let them have ice cream before dinner when they were younger.

Blake poked her head into the room and yawned. "Could you hang out with her for a bit? Clint ran out to get a couple of pizzas. I'm dying to soak in a bubble bath."

"Go for it. We have some catching up to do." Brittany winked at Macy, who giggled.

"Thanks. You guys have fun." Blake turned and walked upstairs.

Macy batted her long eyelashes and smiled, revealing two adorable dimples at the corners of her mouth. "Can I have two scoops of ice cream? Pretty please!"

"Good try, but you have to save room for your dinner."

Macy pursed her lips together and blew raspberries. "Okie dokie."

Brittany playfully tapped her niece on the nose, then kissed it. After filling two soda fountain glasses halfway with the ice cream, she topped them with root beer and handed one to Macy.

"Thank you. Can my friend have a float, too?"

Brittany's stomach lurched. "Is your friend here right now?" She scanned the kitchen, not seeing another soul. Was it just an imaginary friend? Brittany looked around the room. If an evil spirit was to blame, they were in hiding. Although the Nelson sisters could see spirits, the deceased didn't have to reveal themselves at all times. More powerful ghosts could even choose who could see them in a given moment.

Macy put her spoon down and swallowed. "Yes. He is

here, and he wants a yummy root beer float, just like mine."
She picked up her glass and slurped.

"Be careful. Don't drink too fast, or you'll get a brain
freeze, um, an ouchie inside your head." A wave of nausea
hit Brittany. "What does your friend look like?"

The child pulled her glass from her lips and stared across
the room, cocking her head as if she were taking mental notes
of someone's appearance. Brittany shivered. This friend
wasn't imaginary after all.

"Is your friend a boy or a girl?"

Macy shook her head. "He isn't a boy. He is old, like
Daddy."

"What color is his hair? Is it black or yellow?"

Macy shrugged. "He told me not to tell you. He said if I
do what he says, he will get me my very own doggie to be
Willow's best friend. And Willow gets so lonely. No one
plays with her but me."

Brittany's eyes widened, and she held her gurgling
stomach. "Don't talk to that man, Macy. He is not your
friend. He is terrible." It wasn't enough for Parker to come
back and torment the Nelson sisters. He *just* had to befriend
Macy. *Wait! Why did a toddler have the blessing, or in this
case, the curse? This is so messed up.*

Macy kicked and cried. "He is my friend. I want a puppy!
Willow needs a friend, too!" She kicked the footrest on her
booster seat.

"Hey, what's going on here? You can't talk to Aunt Britt
that way, understand? You listen to her and be nice." Clint
walked into the kitchen and set two pizza boxes onto the
table before walking over to Macy, whose eyes filled with
tears.

"Okay, Daddy. I promise to be nice. Sorry, Auntie Britt.
Huggies?"

She leaned in and squeezed Macy's shoulders, but she
struggled to remain calm while her niece finished her ice
cream. Poor kid. None of this was her fault. Parker always

had a way of making a mess of their lives. How on earth did he sneak out of his final resting place?

Clint pulled Brittany aside. "What's going on with her? If you notice anything strange, let me know. I'm so worried."

Brittany nodded. "Her friend isn't a kid. He told her to keep secrets from us. Who do you think that could be?"

Clint's eyes widened, and he shook his head. Drawing a deep breath, he kneeled in front of his daughter and looked her in the eyes. "Is your friend an adult, or are you playing make-believe right now?"

"Is real, Daddy." Macy teared up again, kicking the back of her chair. "Macy never tell lies. Promise!" Her lower lip quivered, turning into a pout.

"It's okay. Just don't talk to him anymore. If he shows up, tell a grown-up. Do you understand?"

Macy nodded, but she hung her head.

Brittany picked up her niece and signed to her. "We love you, Macy Bear. We don't want you to get hurt, okay? Are you going to do what we asked you to?"

The child nodded, lay her head on Brittany's shoulder and began sucking her thumb. Brittany rubbed Macy's back and looked at Clint, who frowned. Brittany suspected she knew what he was thinking. Parker had wreaked havoc in their lives. Now, he was pulling Macy into his web.

"Should we tell Blake what's up now?" Clint asked.

Brittany rubbed her temples. "Give me one day to figure something out. If I don't have an answer by tomorrow night, we'll tell her then. I'm hoping we don't need to pull her in. I'm not sure how she'll take the news."

He nodded and turned to tend to Macy. There had to be a solution to their problem, and Brittany knew where to start. She grabbed a slice of pizza and walked to the living room bookcase. Looking through the titles, most of the books were about Charleston history and gardening, with a few beach reads thrown in for good measure. *Damn it.* There was no sign of their grandmother's book, *The Curse and the Blessing of the Other Side.* Hmm. Where could it be?

25

Blake nudged her and signed. "What are you looking for?"

"Just something light and fun to read on the beach tomorrow. I thought I'd take Macy out to build sandcastles and splash around at the beach. You guys should go do something fun."

Blake smiled. "I'm so glad you're here. We're going to have a great time catching up, and you've already helped me a lot. Thanks for everything."

"No problem. I'm going to crash. It's been a long day. Goodnight."

Chapter 4

B rittany walked upstairs, but she stepped into Blake and Clint's room instead of her own. Invading their privacy was a no-no, but this was an urgent matter. Carefully opening a curio cabinet, she moved a row of knick-knacks out of the way and reached for a worn hardcover book. As she placed her hand on the book's tattered binding, a crystal paperweight shifted and fell onto the floor. The pounding of fast-approaching footsteps thundered up the steps and into her throat. The thud must have resounded downstairs. She prepared for what to tell her sister when she found her sneaking around her bedroom.

The door opened. "Are you okay?" Clint asked. "You're not making it easy for me to keep Blake off your trail." *How embarrassing!*

"I'm just trying to find Granny's book. That paperweight is heavy and almost took out my foot. You could probably murder someone with it."

Clint laughed. "I think it was a wedding gift. Trust me; Blake will never get rid of it. Speaking of my stubborn wife, if you don't want her to know you're in here, you'd better hurry. She's getting ready to put Macy to bed."

Brittany grabbed the book and blew some dust off the top. "Thank God. This is it. I promise to stay out of your bedroom from now on. 'Night.'"

She went to her room and curled up in her favorite chair. The book was a window into their grandmother's young adult life. Most people would have run for the hills after her experiences, but not Granny Mason. She'd embraced her gift for communicating with the dead. Not only had she been able to protect her family by using her abilities, she had also helped many desperate souls find their way to their final resting place. She was a superhero.

A chapter title, *When the Cleansing Ceremony Comes Undone*, caught her eye. *BINGO*. Brittany exhaled.

It's rare, but sometimes a spirit finds a loophole to return to earth. If you find yourself with a hitchhiking specter, return to the location where you conducted the cleansing ceremony. Dig up the letter and tree you planted. Burn them in the last place you saw the deceased alive. All of this must occur during a lunar eclipse with the original ceremony members present.

Brittany's eyelids were heavy. It was time to get some rest. Pulling herself out of the chair, she lay down the book on her nightstand. Stretching, she realized she hadn't heard from Ryan.

She thought about what to say. Every time she started to tell him about Parker's return, she deleted what she'd typed. Ryan couldn't help her from Seattle. She'd spare him the concern.

Brittany: *Hi, sweetie. I love you. I haven't heard from you since I got here. I hope everything is going well with your residency. I'm sure you're knocking your bosses' socks off. I can't wait to see you! XOXO*

She set her phone on top of the book and closed her eyes. Rolling onto her stomach, she thought about Ryan. If he were at the cottage, he would have confronted Parker off the bat. She would finish reading her granny's book tomorrow and learn how to take the demented jerk down peg by peg. No one would get away with messing with Macy!

Light filled Brittany's room the next morning, waking her. She grabbed her cell phone and flipped through her social media feeds, laughing at memes and liking her friends' recent posts. After a few minutes, she was fully awake. *It's time to read again.* She reached for her granny's book, but it wasn't where she'd left it. Did it fall behind the nightstand? She stood up to check, but it wasn't there. Brittany kneeled and looked under the bed. It was gone. *Damn it, Parker!*

"Give the book back. You hear me?" Brittany punched the bed. "Show your face."

The hairs on her arm stood up straight, and a chill trickled down her spine. Someone was staring at her. She turned to see her grandmother standing at the foot of her bed and relaxed. After Granny Mason died, Brittany discovered she could *hear* her grandmother's voice once again. Her low humming comforted Brittany's soul.

"Oh, so glad to see you! Parker's back. He took Blake's copy of your book while I was asleep."

"I know. We got here as soon as we could."

Brittany winced. "You keep saying *we.* Is Papa helping you?"

Granny Mason rubbed her chin. "No. There's someone else." She sighed. "Nan, you may as well come out."

The young blond woman from the graduation ceremony appeared and opened her arms to hug Brittany. She pulled away to allow Brittany to read her lips. "You may as well know it's me, hon. I've missed you Nelson girls and my boys, too!"

Brittany's jaw dropped. "Nancy! That was you in the arena? Why do you look so, um, different?"

"I don't want Clint or Blake to think I'm spying on them. They've started their lives together, but I wanted to see my great-grandchild. I knew there was a strong possibility she would have the gift. Unfortunately, I was right. I wouldn't wish this life on anyone." Nancy grasped Granny Mason's hand.

Brittany gulped, imagining Blake's reaction when she

29

learned about Macy's impending powers. She shifted her weight from foot to foot. "Blake and Clint are going out today. Can you two stick around until I put Macy down for her mid-morning nap?"

The women nodded. "We'll be here," Nancy said.

Brittany changed out of her pajamas and slipped on a pair of shorts and a tank top. She padded down the stairs and into the kitchen.

Macy was sitting in her booster seat, eating grapes. Brittany kissed the toddler's forehead and looked over at Blake. "Hey, sis, what are you and Clint gonna do today?"

"Well, how would you feel about us going away for a night? We don't have any B&B guests scheduled to arrive for the next month, so we thought it would be nice to drive up to Wilmington and check out the antique shops."

Perfect! Brittany's mind raced. That would buy her the time she needed to find a solution. Clint must have planted the idea in Blake's head. She'd have to thank him later. "That's fine with us, isn't it, Macy? We'll bake cookies and blow bubbles in the yard for Willow to chase."

Macy jumped out of her booster seat and pushed Blake toward the door. "Bye. Bye, Mommy! See you later. Love you."

Clint walked into the room, laughing. "Are you sending Mommy away?"

Macy giggled and buried her head into his stomach, pushing him away. "You go, too! Bye, Daddy!"

"Well, okay, then. If you don't want us here, we'll go. Be good for Aunt Britt, okay?" Clint leaned over to kiss Blake. "You ready?"

Blake ran into the living room and grabbed her purse off the sofa. "Text us if you need anything."

Brittany waved her hands. "We'll be fine. We're gonna have a girls' day."

After hugging Macy goodbye, Clint and Blake left the cottage, and Brittany let out a sigh of relief. Hopefully, she could make some progress in getting rid of Parker.

At least her grandmother and Nancy were waiting in the wings to help.

"Let's make cookies now!" Macy danced around the kitchen with a silver princess wand decorated with swirling pink ribbons.

Combining the ingredients in a bowl, Brittany watched her niece. Macy wrinkled her nose and smiled. She was sneaking chocolate chips and dancing in her seat—*hello sugar high, goodbye mid-morning nap.* Brittany couldn't have Macy telling Blake and Clint she'd met her deceased great-grandmothers. No. That wouldn't do. She'd keep the introductions simple.

The gooey cookie dough stuck to the spoon as Brittany dropped heaping spoonsful inches apart onto a cookie sheet. Brittany put the cookies into the oven, and Macy licked her lips. "How long will it take for the cookies to cook?"

Brittany couldn't help laughing. This kid had inherited the Nelson family's sweet tooth. "Probably ten minutes or so. Why don't you go play with Willow in the garden while we wait?"

Macy nodded and opened the door for Willow, who frolicked into the yard, chasing a butterfly. Watching them from the screened-in porch, Brittany remembered playing in the garden with her sisters when they were younger. *Too bad Macy doesn't have any kids her age to play with here.* Maybe Blake and Clint would have another child soon to give Macy a sibling to grow up with, or they could enroll her in a playgroup or preschool program. Brittany realized part of the reason they hadn't been in a rush to do either—from their perspective, Macy hadn't been the easiest child to raise. If she could send Parker away before Blake was any the wiser, it would give them a chance to see how good their spunky daughter was.

Goosebumps prickled up Brittany's arms when she sensed someone was watching her. She turned around to see Nancy standing behind her, smiling. Brittany jumped. "Agh!

31

Nancy! You scared me to death."

"So sorry, hon. I wanted to help you get started with trying to get rid of our, ahem, problem."

A reminder popped up on her phone. *The cookies!* "Hang on. I'll be right back." She went back into the house, grabbed a potholder and retrieved the cookie sheet from the oven.

In the condensation on the oven door's glass section, someone had smeared the words, *Careful, bitch.* The hairs on Brittany's arm stood on end. She couldn't see anyone in her peripheral vision, but she didn't need to guess who had made the snide comment. She drew a deep breath and said a silent prayer before turning around.

"Screw you! I won't let you hurt Macy! Just go back to wherever you've been and leave our family alone." Parker's presence brought back unsettling memories of him groping her after Blake had fallen asleep during a family trip. He'd threatened to kill Brittany if she ever shared the incident with her sister. Parker had invented an alternate reality where Brittany was in love with him. He'd even told Blake that she flirted with him continuously, even though nothing could be further from the truth. Blake had teased her about it, but Brittany had to wonder if some part of Blake believed him. Brittany despised Parker from her very core. Her head spinning, she clutched her stomach to keep her nausea at bay.

Parker materialized, laughing. "You know I don't give up that easily. Unfortunately, I can't pester Blake and her hubby right now since you guys did that silly little cleansing ceremony. That's why I had to wait for them to leave. Thanks so much for playing the hospitable hostess. I know you've always had a thing for me. Why don't we make it happen now that I'm available?" Five years ago, Brittany and her family had banished the evil spirit to the Other Side, or so they'd thought. Why hadn't the ceremony's effect been more permanent?

"Shut up, Parker! Hey, Nancy! We've got company." *Where did Nancy go? She always thinks on her feet.*

"What's grandma going to do? She's dead, too." Parker smirked. "As if that hag could do anything to me."

Nancy snuck up behind him and slipped her cross pendant onto his neck. Flames jutted out around the chain, and Parker's eyes widened as he vanished into a cloud of smoke.

"Where did you find that?" Brittany clutched her heart and pulled out a chair.

Her friend winked. "I might be dead, but this old *hag* still has a few tricks up her sleeve."

Brittany laughed. "Thank goodness for that. Whew! I know that isn't a permanent fix, but I'm glad you bought us some time. I'd better go check on Macy and Willow."

Thankfully, Macy was oblivious to the scene that had taken place inside the cottage. She was playing with Willow near the swing set Clint had built for her that spring. "Macy? Come on inside and bring Willow." The two ran into the kitchen, and Macy yawned. "You look sleepy. Why don't you take a nap? When you wake up, we'll have lunch and cookies for dessert."

Macy blew her bangs out of her eyes and nodded. Willow followed her up the open staircase. When Brittany saw the door to her niece's bedroom close, she looked around the room. "Hey, Nancy, you and Granny can come out now."

Chapter 5

Granny Mason appeared first. She smoothed her skirt and locked her hands together. "Britt, he'll be able to come back in a day or two. We've got to think quick. The only way I know to get rid of him is to reverse the cleansing ceremony and retry it from the beginning."

Brittany put her hands on her hips and shook her head. "But that means Blake would have to get involved because she was here for the first ceremony. I want to spare her the pain of reliving this horror."

"Me, too. I didn't say it was the only way; it's just the only one I know. The only good thing is the cleansing ceremony detached Parker from Blake and Clint." Granny Mason punched her palm. "The bad news is that's why he's coming after you and Macy. Don't worry. I won't let that slimy snake hurt either of you."

Blood pulsated through Brittany's veins, and she rubbed her arms to calm herself. Nothing could happen to Macy, her family's biggest blessing. She wouldn't be able to forgive herself.

"I'm going to look around for the book," Granny Mason said. "In the meantime, can you text Paulene and see if she can come over? Sometimes, she's better at figuring out this nonsense off the cuff than I am."

Brittany pulled her phone out of her pocket and flipped through her contacts. She took a deep breath as she texted Paulene, who agreed to help. The floorboards bowed under

Brittany's pacing feet. Surely, Brittany could get rid of their unwanted visitor without involving Blake. She wasn't ready to give up yet. They had Macy to think of this time. Speaking of which, it was time to wake up the toddler. Brittany ran upstairs to see Macy jumping on her bed, her dark ringlets bouncing.

She jumped into Brittany's arms and giggled. "What we doing today?"

Brittany smiled back at Macy as she carried her niece downstairs to the kitchen. "Some nice ladies are going to hang out with us this afternoon. They're helping me take care of some things. But first, we're going to have lunch and some of those yummy cookies!"

"Yay!" Macy climbed up into her booster seat and drummed her fingers on the table.

Brittany fixed peanut butter and jelly sandwiches and cut up an apple for them to share. Her niece playfully ate her lunch, clapping her hands. When Brittany handed Macy a cookie, she took a bite and offered one to Brittany. This kid melted her heart in so many ways. Out of the corner of her eye, she saw Nancy watching them, smiling. "Hey, you can come over here. I told Miss Macy that we'd have some visitors today."

Nancy glided across the room and patted Macy on the head. "I've known your aunt for a long time. I'm glad to meet you, young lady."

Macy's eyes sparkled as she revealed her chocolate-covered teeth. "Want a cookie?"

Nancy giggled. "Thank you, but heavens no. I've gotta keep my girlish figure." She winked at Brittany, who rolled her eyes.

The doorbell notification appeared on Brittany's phone, and she ran to open the door. On the other side stood Paulene, decked out in a flowing crimson pants suit so dark it was almost black. Emerald rings adorned each of her fingers. The older woman had pulled her black and silver hair into a French twist, held in place with a single red and gold

35

chopstick, topped with a peacock feather. How could Brittany have forgotten Paulene's intense sense of fashion?

"Hi, there. Look who I found walking around in the front yard." Paulene smiled, moving to the side, with Granny Mason standing behind her. Her simple blue shift dress and pearls didn't match her friend's outlandish outfit. Their personalities were just as different as their wardrobe.

Granny Mason locked eyes with Brittany and smiled. "I didn't find the book, but we'll figure out something. Is Nan still around?"

"Yeah. She's in the kitchen with Macy. By the way, don't call each other by name. I don't want Macy to talk about you to Blake and worry her."

Granny Mason twisted an imaginary key to lock her lips and pretended to throw it away. Paulene nodded and pulled an invisible zipper across her lips. The women trooped into the kitchen where Nancy sat, watching Macy with an adoring smile. Brittany brushed cookie crumbs off the child's face and asked her to watch television while the adults chatted.

"Cartoons, cartoons!" Macy hopped from the kitchen to the living room and crashed onto the sofa. Brittany flipped through the streaming networks until she found Macy's favorite show about cats.

"Stay here and be a good girl. We'll go outside and play later, okay?"

Macy nodded, already laser-focused on the screen. Brittany kissed her niece's forehead and left the room to join the other women at the kitchen table.

Paulene pulled a chair out for her. "C'mon. Tell us what's been going on."

Brittany pushed her hair out of her face and filled them in on Parker's recent antics. Her heart was racing, but she made sure not to leave out any details that might help them find a solution. These were some of the most brilliant women she'd ever met, so if anyone could send Parker back, it would be them.

"Well, we can't keep throwing the cross pendant around his neck. He'll eventually figure out a way around that." Granny Mason wrapped her index finger around her lip.

Parker had tormented Blake and their family right before she had married Clint. They thought they had sent him on to his final resting place, and, as the old Southern saying goes, *they hadn't seen hide nor hair of him* in the past five years. What had changed?

Paulene waved her hand to get Brittany's attention. "You're not saying much, Brittany. What are you thinking about? Anything you've noticed might help us figure out a means to an end for Parker."

She shrugged. "I'm just trying to figure out how he squirmed his way back. I thought that once you banished a spirit, it was for good."

Granny Mason nodded. "That's always been my experience, but it's not completely unheard of for a spirit to come back."

"Same here." Paulene winced. "I know of one way we can guarantee that he'll never come back, but it's risky. It should be our last resort, or someone could get hurt."

Granny Mason put out her hand. "Let's see what else we can cook up first."

Brittany's text notification sounded. It was Blake. She excused herself and stepped out onto the screened-in porch to clear her head.

Blake: *Hey! Is everything going okay? Is Macy behaving?*

Brittany: *She's been a perfect angel...just watching cartoons right now.*

Blake: *Awesome! Would you mind if we stayed here for a few more nights? We didn't realize how badly we needed a break.*

Brittany smiled, replying that they should stay as long as they wanted. She walked back into the house. "Good news, ladies. They're staying in Wilmington longer than expected." She put her hands together and touched them to her lips.

"Hallelujah! They're working on making us another great-grandbaby." Nancy laughed, elbowing Julia Caroline.

Brittany's cheeks flushed. Not that she'd mind having another niece or nephew. Honestly, though, her sister's text was better than *good*. It meant that she had even more time to solve the latest mystery on Palm Court. She'd better get to it.

Granny Mason turned to Brittany. "You need to start by digging up the letter, picture, and tree that Blake planted. Ask Elaina and your Mom to come for the week. We'll need their help to undo the cleansing ceremony since they were here the first time. There's safety and strength in numbers. They'll jump at the chance to see Macy."

As she dialed her Mom's phone number for a video chat, she knew her grandmother was right. Her sister and Mom would be excited to spend time with Macy. Furthermore, they'd love to kick Parker's ass a second time. Brittany anticipated that herself.

"Hey, can you and Elaina come to the island?" Brittany signed. The last thing she wanted was to beg her mom and sister to drive six hours to help her exterminate a pest. "We have an unwanted visitor at the cottage."

"We can come, but is everything okay?"

"Not really. Parker is back. We don't know why or how. I'm trying to keep Blake from finding out. I think the stress might kill her this time."

Her mom sighed. "I had a feeling it might be too good to be true when he vanished after the cleansing ceremony. We'll leave first thing in the morning. Please be careful."

A light flashed on Brittany's phone, so she scrolled through her apps to see if she had missed a call or text from Ryan, but no such luck. She'd received a call from an unknown number while she'd been on the video call with her mom. The caller had left a voicemail, but her voice-to-text app couldn't transcribe the message. Exhausted from Parker's return, she dismissed it. She'd have her mom or sister listen to it when they arrived in the morning.

Chapter 6

Later that afternoon, Brittany walked out to the garden, shovel in hand. She struck the hard-packed soil surrounding the roots of the dogwood tree Blake had planted. Brittany kneeled beside the tree and continued to move the sandy earth aside as she looked for the items her sister had buried. A few inches into the ground, her hands brushed across a wooden box—fingers crossed—the letter and picture were inside, nestled on a piece of tissue paper.

She removed the lid, revealing a photograph of Parker and a folded piece of paper. Brittany shivered. Not only did she hate getting her hands dirty, but she also didn't want to relive the night before Blake and Clint's wedding. Parker had tormented the entire family on so many levels, especially Blake. She reminded herself she needed to suck it up and keep going. Her niece's safety, and her own, were at stake. She wiped her brow and unfolded the letter, but it was blank, not even a trace of the permanent marker. The paper was crisp and pure white, good as new. How could that be? She had watched her sister write several paragraphs. Brittany examined the photograph again. It was in perfect condition, with no sign of fading or discoloration. Trying to preserve the tree, she reseeded the roots and sprayed the earth with the adjacent water hose.

Granny Mason appeared beside her. "Did you find everything?"

Brittany nodded and handed her the box. "Look at the

letter. I don't get it."

Her grandmother frowned. "He must have counteracted the spell. That boy keeps surprising me. I didn't give him enough credit."

"None of us have, but there has to be something we can do." Brittany groaned and kicked the ground.

"Your mom and Elaina will be here tomorrow. We'll fill them in and get ready for when Blake comes home. Then, we can quickly undo the cleansing ceremony and try it again over the weekend. There's supposed to be a lunar eclipse. If we wait, we won't get another chance for quite some time."

Brittany interrupted her. "But we don't want Blake to find out what's going on. Are we just going to give up?"

"If Paulene doesn't know of a safe solution, we're going to go with the tried and true." Granny Mason put her hand on Brittany's shoulder. "I love you, child. I just don't want this to get out of hand. I know you feel the same way."

"Totally, but I'm dreading telling Blake I've been hiding something from her. When we were kids, we made a pact that we wouldn't ever lie to each other. As far as I know, we haven't."

Granny Mason smiled. "I'm proud that you can say that. You and your sisters have grown up into such lovely women."

"We had several great role models, most of all, you and Mom." Brittany hugged her grandmother.

Paulene tapped Brittany on the shoulder and said goodbye.

"Thanks so much for coming. We're regrouping. If you think of something, please call me. If not, we'll let you know when we're going to host the ceremony."

Paulene nodded and wished them luck before walking along the garden path to the driveway and getting into her car.

"We're going to need it," Brittany mumbled under her breath and walked back into the cottage to check on Macy, who had fallen asleep on the living room sofa.

Nancy's eyes danced as she stared at the child. "I thank God for allowing me to be part of her life in a small way. Granted, it's not the same as being alive. I wish I could take her on vacation or even just out to lunch, but this is better than nothing."

A tear rolled down Brittany's cheek. "She's lucky to have you around. I'm glad you've had this time with her." She wiped her eyes with her sleeve. "I'll leave you here with her while I make dinner."

The plump shrimp and crisp zucchini sizzled in the avocado oil on the stove. The food filled the kitchen with a comforting scent—one Brittany remembered well from her childhood summers at the cottage. Of course, Granny Mason would have used lard, not avocado oil, but close enough. She and her sisters had loved spending time with Granny Mason. She was their hero.

Nancy walked into the kitchen and tilted her head. "Don't worry. Blake will understand you were trying to protect her emotional wellbeing. She would've done the same for you."

Brittany tried to smile and reassure herself. "I hope so. Anyway, we don't have much of a choice but to tell her. Granny thinks it's best."

Nancy nodded and blew her a kiss before disappearing into an iridescent mist. She'd served as Blake's navigator to the paranormal world during Parker's first haunting. Her sister would celebrate when she knew that Nancy had returned.

Lowering the stove heat, Brittany walked into the living room and carried Macy to her booster seat in the kitchen. Her niece bounced up and down and looked over to where Nancy had been standing. "Where your friends go?"

"Sweetie, they had to leave."

"To go back to Heaven?" Macy batted her eyelashes.

Brittany almost dropped the plates she had filled. How did Macy know Granny Mason and Nancy were dead, and how should she respond to her niece's question? Drawing a deep breath, she placed her hand on Macy's shoulder. "What do you mean?"

"My friend told me," Macy said, her mouth full of shrimp.

Brittany gasped. Her stomach flipped and flopped, churned and turned. But she needed answers, even if they weren't to her liking.

"He was in my dreams. He said they came from Heaven, and I didn't need to listen to them."

"No! He was wrong about who you should listen to. He is bad. Please promise not to listen to him. Do you understand?"

Macy nodded, spooning another bite of shrimp into her mouth. How could Parker mess with this child? His spirit was evil, but surely, he wouldn't harm Macy. He was just trying to get under Brittany's skin so she would tell Blake what was happening. Once a narcissist, always a narcissist.

The day had gotten away from her. It was 7:45, almost time to send Macy to bed. Her niece didn't say another word during dinner, and Brittany was too tired to make conversation. When Macy rubbed her eyes halfway through the meal, Brittany asked her if she'd finished eating. The child nodded and toddled off to the bathroom and then her bedroom, waiting to be tucked into bed. Willow jumped up beside her and cuddled into her usual spot at the foot of the bed. Brittany kissed her niece and petted the dog's head before shutting off the light.

Settling into bed, Brittany yawned. It was only 8:30, but she couldn't keep her eyes open. Why hadn't Ryan texted her yet? She tried calling him for a video chat, but he didn't answer, so she sent him another text.

Brittany: Hey, babe. I'm sure you're just busy, but I haven't talked to you since I've been in South Carolina. Please let me know you're okay. I love you! Talk to you in the morning. :)

She grimaced. If she didn't hear from him the next day,

she'd text his family to see if they'd heard from him. Her phone dropped out of her hand and hit her face—she had fallen asleep mid-thought! *I am getting old, or at least boring.* As Brittany drifted off to sleep, she dreamed about Ryan. Like a top, he spun in circles, spinning faster with each revolution and reaching out to her for help. No matter what Brittany tried, she couldn't stop him. She woke in a sweat, her pulse racing. There was something so real about the dream. What did it mean? Was he okay? She checked the time; it was midnight. His parents and brothers would be asleep. It would have to wait until the morning, which meant this would be a long night.

Chapter 7

As Brittany stirred in bed the next morning, glare from approaching headlights filled her room. Elaina and their mom had arrived. She tiptoed down the steps, careful not to wake Macy. After checking her reflection in the entryway hall mirror, she greeted them outside. "I'm so relieved you guys are here!"

Elaina slammed the trunk shut, placing a large suitcase on the ground. "We drove all night. We couldn't stand the thought of that jerk causing our family any more grief. How can we get rid of his sorry ass?"

"We haven't found a solution that I like. Granny thinks we're gonna have to tell Blake." Brittany wrapped her arms around herself, attempting to find some comfort at the thought of Blake's reaction.

Susan scowled. "I hate anyone who tries to hurt my girls."

Elaina put her head into her palms. "This whole situation sucks so bad. I can't believe Parker is back."

Parker appeared on the front porch, wearing his trademark smirk. "Damn straight. I'm here."

Brittany locked eyes with him. "You should know this by now. You're not welcome here. Blake isn't here, and even if she was, she has no interest in seeing you." She pulled out her cell phone and began reading excerpts from the Bible, covering verses from Genesis to Revelations. His evil sneer didn't waver until she read scripture from the Book of Mark.

And he said to them, this kind cannot be driven out by anything but prayer.

Susan, who didn't have the gift to see spirits herself, depended on her daughters to know the situation's intensity. She grabbed their hands. "Then, let's pray."

They formed a circle, holding hands and bowing their heads. Brittany began speaking with her voice, "Dear Lord, please help us return this evil spirit to where he's been for the past five years. We rely on your wisdom and strength and ask for your protection during this trial in our lives. In Jesus' name, Amen."

A blast of cold wind blew loose pieces of Brittany's hair into her mouth. She opened her eyes. Parker had disappeared. The residual imprint of where he'd stood continued fading, but the weight on her chest had lightened. During his last reign of terror, prayer alone hadn't kept him away. Maybe this time would be different. She had a strong faith in God, but she was also a realist. Sometimes, terrible things happened to good people, believers and nonbelievers alike. That being said, God was good, and He was on their side—that much was for sure.

Brittany grabbed her mom's suitcase, and they walked into the house. "C'mon into the cottage. Y'all must be exhausted from the drive and, well, all of this. Are you hungry?"

Elaina clutched her stomach, and everyone laughed. "I guess I am. I'll whip up some pancakes if one of you wants to go wake up Macy."

Susan's eyes lit up. "Let me go get her. I've missed my little girl." Her feet pounded up the steps. Brittany and Elaina smiled at each other. It had been hard on their mom living six hours away from her only grandchild, but she made the most of it when they were together.

Their mom returned to the kitchen without Macy in tow. "She wasn't in her room. Have you seen her? Did she slip past me somehow?" Susan ran back upstairs, and when she hadn't returned a few minutes later, Brittany checked on her.

45

Susan stood in Macy's room, with tears streaming down her face. "I can't find Macy. Where could she be? Does she have a hiding spot, a closet or something?" Susan wiped a tear from the corner of her eye.

Brittany shook her head. "Not that I'm aware of. You keep looking in the house. I'm going outside to make sure she isn't playing with Willow." As the words left her mouth, her jaw trembled. Macy wasn't the type to hide or go off on her own. She didn't like being alone.

Elaina stopped Brittany on her way to the kitchen door. "You didn't find her?"

"No," Brittany signed. "Mom's still looking upstairs. I'm gonna go check the garden." *Macy has to be out there.*

"I'm coming with you." Elaina's eyes widened as she turned off the stove.

Willow jumped up onto Brittany when they stepped outside, sending her mind spinning. In between barks, the typically docile dog ran in circles. Brittany opened the door to the gardening shed, but no one was inside. She turned back to see her sister clutching Macy's favorite stuffed dog, which had four little red smears on its stomach.

Brittany's blood ran cold. Did Parker take her niece? How far could a ghost take a child? She had no choice but to tell Blake what was going on now that Macy was missing. How could she have allowed this to happen? The ground tilted underneath her, forcing her to sit down to steady her body. "I'm texting Clint. He can get his officers out looking for her. I can't tell Blake her daughter is missing through a text or even a video call. I just can't."

Susan's rubbed her red, puffy eyes and wrapped her arm around Brittany. "We'll find her. We have to."

At this moment, Brittany wished she could pick up the phone and call Clint. She'd never wanted to hear her brother-in-law's voice so much in her life. A video call wouldn't work because he didn't speak sign language, and reading lips wasn't possible on a small screen. Texting didn't seem right, but it was all she had. Struggling to see her phone screen through the tears, she fumbled out the words.

Brittany: Macy is missing. Mom and Elaina are here with me. We think Parker may have taken her. What can we do?

This is totally my fault. Brittany berated herself for not telling Blake about Parker from the very beginning. Her sister may have been able to work something out sooner since she had more experience dealing with the evil spirit. She sniffed and wiped her eyes on the sleeves of her T-shirt. Her stomach knotted as she watched three dots bouncing at the bottom of her phone screen, indicating Clint's typing.

Clint: What?! Let me get the team on this right away. Hang tight. I'll start a group text.

A burning sensation boiled from the pit of Brittany's stomach and up into her throat. She gulped, hoping to extinguish the flames. A light flashed on her phone, grabbing her attention.

Clint: Shane and Roger are part of this text thread now. They're heading your way. Can you tell us everything you know, starting with when you last saw her?

Brittany wiped her eyes and replayed the past day's events. Why did this happen to Macy? Where did Parker take her? How could she get her back?

Brittany: I tucked her in at around eight last night. She was wearing her pajamas with pink and green starfish on them. She said her prayers and asked for a bedtime story. Then I kissed her goodnight. It was a very typical evening. I didn't notice anything out of the ordinary until Mom and Elaina got here around 6:30 this morning. I ran downstairs to let them into the house. That's when we saw Parker.

Clint: So, you didn't see her this morning?

Brittany winced. Why hadn't she checked on Macy before running downstairs? That was irresponsible.

Brittany: No. I'm so sorry. I didn't want Mom or Elaina to wake up Macy. I was trying to beat them to the punch.

The three dots danced along the bottom of her screen,

disappeared and reappeared as if Clint couldn't decide what else to say. Finally, he responded again.

Clint: "Okay. Can you think of anything else that might help us find her?

Her throat tightened like it was full of cotton balls; she struggled to clear her mind enough to answer him.

Brittany: Elaina found her stuffed dog in the garden. There are some little red smudges on its belly.

Clint: No…

Brittany: Clint, I will do everything I can to find her.

The three dots returned but disappeared again. Brittany's pulse sped out of control until Clint's team arrived. Drawing a deep breath, she shook the officers' hands. She recognized them from various family events Clint and Blake had hosted at the cottage, which helped her feel slightly more at ease while talking to them.

"Can we see the stuffed animal?" Roger asked.

Elaina walked over and handed it to him. "See these little red marks? Could these be her fingerprints?" She dabbed her eyes with a tissue and sniffed.

He inspected the toy and twisted his mouth. "It might not be blood; try not to worry. We'll have the lab test it. Does Macy have a favorite playground or spot on the beach?"

Susan huffed. "A three-year-old couldn't walk to any of those places by herself."

Roger adjusted his sunglasses. "Ma'am. We're just considering the possibilities. We love Macy, too, and we'd love nothing more than to find her playing at a park right now."

"I'm sorry. I'm beyond worried." Susan went inside to get a notepad and jotted down Macy's favorite places on the island.

When she returned, Roger clasped her hand in his. "We're going to do everything we can to find her and bring her back home today."

Susan nodded, and tears spilled out of her eyes as she

thanked him.

After they left, Brittany held her hand to her chest and closed her eyes, trying to calm herself. How could this have happened? Macy deserved a caretaker who would protect her at all costs. That had been her job. It shouldn't have been so hard. Blake would never forgive her; she'd never forgive herself. This is precisely why she shouldn't have kids. No one deserved a mom who couldn't keep them safe.

Chapter 8

The decking boards on the front porch seared Brittany's bare feet, but she couldn't just sit inside while waiting for Clint and Blake's return. Pacing back and forth, she ran through what to say to her sister about Macy's disappearance. None of the words she strung together sounded apologetic or compassionate enough for the situation. Unfortunately, there wasn't a greeting card with the message, "Please forgive me for losing your child. P.S. Your ex is a psychotic ghost who is hell-bent on ruining our lives." Breathe, in, out, in and out, in and…Clint's old Jeep Wrangler flew down Palm Court, flinging sand and loose shells into nearby yards. He swerved the vehicle into the yard, missing the driveway altogether. *Ready or not, they're home.*

Brittany twisted her hands and said a silent prayer for her niece's safety. Looking up to the sky, she didn't see Blake walking onto the porch. The thud of Blake's hard-shell suitcase shook the decking boards beneath Brittany's feet. Blake's hands flew through the air at a rapid pace. "What the hell, Britt? How could you be so effing irresponsible? You *shouldn't* have kids. You'd just lose them."

Ouch! Brittany's heart sank as she examined her sister's clenched jaw and red puffy eyes. She braced herself, expecting Blake to hit her at any moment.

"Why aren't you answering me?" Blake got in her face and locked eyes with her. "What happened? Where is she?"

Blake reached out and shook Brittany's body, which stung under her sister's firm grip. Looking at her hands, Blake let go and cried out.

Brittany stepped back as tears filled her eyes. "I'm so sorry. I should have told you about Parker from the beginning. I didn't…"

Blake's eyes widened. "Parker? Who said anything about Parker?"

"Clint didn't tell you?" Brittany asked, looking around for her brother-in-law, who was on his phone, presumably talking to his officers about Macy.

Her sister stumbled backward into a seated position, muttering the word "no" repeatedly. Her eyes darkened. "Tell me everything."

I guess Clint was hoping for a miracle, like the rest of us. We were both wrong, so very wrong. Brittany told Blake how Parker had appeared and threatened her and that she'd figured out he was behind Macy's odd and destructive behavior.

"My poor little angel," Blake whispered. "How am I going to find her?"

Brittany threw her arms around her sister, squeezing her but pulled back to sign, "I was responsible for Macy. I won't rest until I find her." She climbed into her car and threw it into drive. Her phone vibrated in her pocket; the amber alert for Macy popped up on the screen. Brittany sobbed. She'd never known a child who had gone missing. Macy was the light of the Nelson family's lives. Reading the alert made it too real.

Driving down the island's main thoroughfare, she blinked away tears and spent the day checking every house, hoping someone had found the child. Because Clint was the police chief, most people knew Macy from town events and were distraught when they heard about her disappearance.

One neighbor, whose son played with Macy every Saturday, mentioned a tunnel that island children liked to crawl inside, even though they shouldn't. She gave Brittany detailed directions on how to find it. Jumping into her car again, she drove to the center of the island, where the Spanish moss wound itself into knots from tree to tree, creating an eerie web.

Brittany shuddered, taking in the perfect setting for a scary movie, not a place where she'd expect to find children playing. She parked her car and explored the nooks and crannies of the dark wooded street. Why would anyone allow their children to come here under any circumstance? *Had she taken a wrong turn?* Suddenly, the hair on her arms rose, and a prickling sensation trickled down her spine. Shivering, she scanned the area for any signs of Parker. About 50 feet away, the twisted tree roots created a natural platform that supported a narrow, rusted culvert.

Looking at the tunnel entrance, Brittany became light-headed. There stood Macy, holding Parker's hand, waving at her through a dark veil of moss. "Auntie Britt! Come play with me and my friend!" Parker waved, sneering as he pulled the child through the opening of the culvert. She was so close to getting Macy back from the demented spirit! *What are you waiting for? Run!*

"Macy! Don't go anywhere! I'm coming!" Brittany ran in long strides, making her way to the tunnel. She pushed twisted vines and prickly leaves aside, climbing inside, unable to see more than a foot in front of her. Rocks jabbed and sliced her hands and knees. After a few minutes, she reached the end and pulled herself outside.

The contrast of the dark tunnel and the bright sky made her eyes throb. She blinked and refocused on the scene in front of her—the marshy banks of the Intracoastal Waterway. How had she ended up here? Brittany scanned the shoreline, but there were no signs of Macy or Parker. Where did they go? Sure, Parker could vanish into thin air, but a human child couldn't. She texted Clint and his team to let them know she had seen Macy. *I should have texted them earlier, but I thought I'd catch up with Parker.* Brittany screamed. No matter what decision she made, it wasn't the right one. The malevolent spirit had outsmarted her once again.

Clint and Shane texted her when they arrived, and the three of them took separate paths. Walking in circles for more than three hours, she had to admit defeat and started back to her car. Sore and frustrated, she sat down and lay her head on the steering wheel, crying out of concern for her niece. *Poor kid.* She was so young and trusting. By some miracle, Macy had looked like she was in good health and clean, considering she had been kidnapped and was doing God knows what. She had called Parker her "friend." That gave Brittany some hope. While Parker did not have a shred of compassion in his black, dead heart, she could count on him to calculate that he needed to keep Macy alive and well for now.

Lifting her head, Brittany turned on the headlights, which radiated onto the dash, illuminating a crumpled piece of paper, which she unfolded.

Please pass my regards on to Clint and Blake. They sure made an adorable child. Macy and I are having a great time together for now, but if Blake wants to keep it that way, she needs to meet me alone under the full moon at midnight on Sunday. If I see anyone else is with her, she'll never see her little girl again, and I won't be sad about that. Nope—I'll have a good laugh at her expense.

Brittany wadded up the note and threw it into the passenger-side floorboard. Parker had kidnapped Macy under her watch. It was her responsibility to find her niece. She rolled down her windows and clenched her fists. "Parker, if you can hear me, you'd better not hurt Macy. If you do, you will spend eternity regretting it. I'll make it my purpose in life and death to make you suffer." As she put the car into drive, a tingle went down her spine—a sensation she often experienced just before Parker appeared. She slammed on the brakes. She looked around for Macy, but it was no use. The darkened canopy had turned the forest into an abyss.

Then, the tears came. She'd gotten so close to getting

Macy back, but Parker had outsmarted her. How did he stay a step ahead? They outnumbered him ten to one. He had to have someone working with him, but who? Why would they bother?

The glow of a text notification lit up her entire car.

Blake: *Come on home. It's getting late. We've got to talk.*

Acid bubbled up from Brittany's stomach, burning her throat. What else could Blake say? Didn't she know that Brittany felt bad enough already? Her knuckles turned white, gripping the steering wheel. *I need a cocktail and a hundred hours of sleep.* Pulling into the driveway, she groaned. Another piece of bad news might send her over the edge, but there was no choice. She had to go into the cottage. Looking into her rearview mirror, she jumped at the sight of her reflection. Blood seeped from a gash across her cheekbone; bits of leaves and moss poked up throughout her knotted hair. She pulled a clean tissue out of her glove compartment and applied pressure to the wound. A sharp pain radiated from her cheek. Brittany looked into the mirror to see it was black and blue. Cuts and scrapes covered her arms and legs. There wasn't time to feel sorry for herself. She needed to get inside, so she pulled her hair out of the turquoise ponytail holder she'd been wearing, combed it with her fingers and pulled it back again. Taking one last look at herself, she sighed. Disheveled was the best she could do tonight.

Chapter 9

Brittany trudged into the cottage with her head hung low, her sweaty palms hanging at her side. Closing the door behind her, she felt the floor shake as if footsteps were coming from the kitchen. *Great.*

Susan burst into the room. "Oh, my goodness! Where have you been? I've been so worried about you!" She hugged Brittany tightly. After she let go, her eyes widened. "What on earth happened to you? Are you okay?"

"Mom, I'm sorry, but I can't even begin to explain everything now. I'm exhausted, heartbroken, and I still don't have a clue where Macy could be…" Brittany began sobbing. "Poor kid. I'm so sorry I've ruined everyone's lives. I need to lie down before I collapse."

Susan reached out to her, but Brittany turned away and ran upstairs and into her bedroom, locking the door behind her. Deep in her thoughts, she didn't bother turning on the light before jumping into bed. As Brittany rolled onto her side, her body came into contact with someone. Paralyzed in fear, she couldn't even scream. The mattress shifted as if the person had gotten out of bed. When the overhead light came on, it took her eyes a moment to focus. It was Ryan! Why was he here? He was supposed to be across the country, saving lives, but there he was, his deep blue eyes widening with concern.

After catching her breath, she signed frantically, "Holy crap! You scared the hell out of me. I almost had a heart attack. I thought you were Parker."

Ryan frowned, caressing her cheek with his hand. "I'm so sorry. You're safe." He looked her up and down, pulling a leaf out of her hair. "What is going on? Are you hurt?"

She fell into his arms and wept. Her body trembling, he held her upright and kissed her forehead. He then gently held her at arm's length, examined her wounds and gulped. "Good thing I came back early. I'll be right back." He returned with a first aid kit and cleaned and treated each of the cuts. "Now, tell me what happened."

Brittany's lips quivered as she recounted the horrors she'd experienced since arriving in South Carolina. Ryan shook his head in silence. His mouth twitched, but no words came. Instead, he helped her to bed and assured her he'd be right back. Staring at the faded unicorn poster on her wall, she suspected he was talking to Blake, but she couldn't bring herself to join them. The trying day had tested her limits; she couldn't bear additional pain. Sure, Brittany wasn't Macy's mother, but she loved this child more than she'd ever loved anyone. It killed her that Parker had her in his clutches.

Ryan returned with a sandwich and a glass of water. "You need this so you can sleep well tonight. Eat up."

She wasn't hungry, but she knew he would kick into doctor mode again and tell her why she needed to rehydrate and consume some calories. After she ate, he brought in a damp washcloth and helped her clean up from her misadventure. The cold water helped calm her nerves, and when he tucked her into bed, she drifted off into a deep sleep.

At four a.m., she couldn't sleep any longer, so she went downstairs to get a drink. Susan sat in the kitchen, drinking a cup of tea. "Please tell me everything, honey. I know this has been hard on you. I was so worried about you and Macy. I didn't sleep a wink."

Brittany explained the previous day's events to her mom, whose eyes brimmed with tears.

"I didn't want to come home without her, but I couldn't

take any more last night." Brittany looked at the floor and fought the urge to cry again.

Susan lifted Brittany's chin. "None of this is your fault. You know that, right? Blake was just upset, and she said some things she didn't mean. She loves you. We'll work together to find Macy."

Brittany prayed her mom was right. Blake could hold a grudge with the best of them. But that didn't matter; her sister could hate her for the rest of their lives if need be. All she wanted was to find her niece safe and sound.

"Well, now that Blake knows, we can undo the cleansing ceremony. The lunar eclipse is on Saturday. Hopefully, everything will go back to normal after that."

Susan nodded. "That's what we all want. You did the right thing by asking us to come here." She held Brittany's hand and kissed it. "It's still so early. Why don't you get some more shuteye? It's going to be another long day."

"Same goes for you, Mom. See you in a few hours." Brittany walked back upstairs and curled up in bed with Ryan.

He mumbled and opened his eyes. "You're so beautiful. I'm the luckiest man in the world. I'm glad I could transfer here to be with you when I'm not at the hospital."

"Transfer? You're working here?"

"Yeah. My supervisor was able to get me a residency in Charleston. Apparently, my hospital in Seattle is part of the same medical system as the one here."

Brittany wiped a tear from her eye. "Thank God! I'm so grateful!"

In the morning, Brittany walked down the steps, planning to make breakfast for everyone. She dreaded the necessary but inevitable conversation with Blake. To her surprise, her sister came into the house carrying three bags filled with takeout boxes.

"I come bearing a peace offering. How do Acme's shrimp and grits sound?" Blake's lips curled into a half-smile, but her weary eyes told a different story.

Brittany patted her sister's shoulder. "It sounds delicious, but I'm so sorry about Macy. I regret not checking on her that morning. You have every right to be pissed off. Believe me; I'm angry with myself." Tears rolled down her cheeks. "I pray that she's okay."

"Me, too, but I don't blame you. I would have done the same thing if it had meant letting her sleep a little later. You did nothing wrong. I'm sorry."

Brittany sniffed, dabbed her eyes and cleared her throat. "I saw Macy and Parker yesterday. I followed them, but I guess I wasn't quick enough. He led me on one of his famous wild goose chases." She continued explaining the horrific events and the letter he'd left for Blake.

"Did she look okay? Was she hurt?" Blake clenched her fists.

"Surprisingly, she seemed happy and in good shape."

Blake sighed. "Thank God! Can I see the letter?"

"Yep. It's in my car. Be right back." Brittany stepped outside to retrieve the crumpled paper from her car. *Damn it!* Parker was trying to destroy their lives again. The last time, he'd killed Nancy and hurt Blake and Clint multiple times. He just couldn't hurt anyone this time. She looked up into the sky. *Please, God, don't let Parker hurt Macy.*

Walking into the house, she exhaled, pushing negative energy out of her body. She handed the letter to Blake and sat down at the table. Watching her sister's face fall made Brittany's heart sink. Undoing the cleansing ceremony had to work.

"Are you going to meet him?" Brittany asked.

Blake threw her hands in the air. "If the cleansing ceremony doesn't work, what choice do I have? I have to protect Macy."

Brittany pursed her lips. "Let's walk on the beach to clear

our heads and see if any ideas occur to us. I'll leave a note for everyone." She jotted a short note on the dry erase board on the fridge and slipped on her shoes. Blake was in a trance. "Are you up for a walk?"

"Yeah. Fresh air would be nice. I'll put the food up, and then I'll be ready."

"Shoot! I forgot about breakfast," Brittany said. "Well, we can burn some calories before we eat. C'mon."

Chapter 10

The water misted Brittany's feet as she walked along the shoreline with her sister. She hoped the salty air would help calm their nerves or at least relieve some of the pressure that prevented them from thinking clearly. Seagulls soared over the sparkling gray water in loose formation.

She squinted, shielding her eyes with her hand. "Are you up to trying to undo the cleansing ceremony late tonight, early tomorrow morning? The eclipse should be at its peak between 12:45 and 1:15."

"As ready as I'll ever be. I haven't slept since Macy's been gone. If he hurts her…" Blake's face turned red, and she fell to her knees, crying. In between sobs, she got some words out, "My baby's got to be okay."

What if she's not? Trembling, Brittany kneeled, huddled in close with Blake and bowed her head. "Dear God, please watch over Macy and help us bring her home safely very soon. Amen." Brittany opened her eyes, the glare burning them. "We need Granny and Nancy."

"Yeah. I tried reaching them last night, but they didn't show. Wait a minute…" Blake stared just past her. "Parker's at the cottage."

"What?" Brittany turned, staring past the dunes. "How can you see that far?"

"It's not a matter of seeing." Blake rubbed her head. "I can feel a migraine coming on. He's definitely there. We need to go now." Blake took off running.

"What are we going to do or say?" Brittany yelled. She finally caught up with Blake at the edge of Palm Court. "You can't just bust in there without a plan."

Blake spun around. "Okay. What do you suggest?" Then, she leaned over, placing her hand on her knees, and groaned.

"Are you alright?"

Blake looked up at Brittany. "I think so; I just had a sharp stomach cramp. Oh, no!" She ran over to the bushes and threw up.

Brittany cringed. She didn't deal with puking very well, but her sister needed her. Thankfully, Blake came back, and the color returned to her face. "I'm good now; tell me your plan."

"Follow me!" Brittany ran to the garden shed and picked up a pair of shears.

Blake narrowed her eyes and tilted her head. "We're going to stab him?"

"No, silly." Brittany walked over to Granny Mason's white rose bushes and clipped off ten flowers. "White roses suck out the negative energy in the room. During medieval times, people grew this species to bring calm and well-being to everyone who saw or smelled them."

Blake's jaw dropped. "How do you know all of that?"

"You're not the only one who read Granny's book. Tuck half of these in your hair." Brittany used the bobby pins, which had been holding her growing bangs in place, to secure a couple, and put the rest inside the plaits of her French braid. "I feel ridiculous, but hopefully, this will work."

"Let's go find out," Blake said, walking into the cottage.

Brittany clenched her jaw and followed her sister, bracing herself for the worst. But there was an odd stillness, emptiness to the house. "I don't think he's here."

Blake walked back into the room, shaking and clutching a piece of paper. "But he was."

"What does it say?" Brittany sat down on the living room floor, folding her legs under herself. Blake held the letter out

61

to Brittany, who pulled it out of her sister's trembling hands.

Dearest Blake, I hope your sister got the message to you. Be there Sunday, or you won't ever see your little girl ever again. Remember, no one else can come with you, or you'll regret it.

"Damn it!" Brittany slammed her hand on the floor. "He'd better not hurt her. I'll destroy him! He'll just wish he was burning for all eternity!"

Blake stared off in the distance, but she shook her head. "I just want Macy back. That's the only thing that matters. We need to gather everything for tonight. Hopefully, the reversal of the cleansing ceremony will work, and Macy will be home for good. Can you text Paulene and let her know we need her tonight?"

"I'm on it right now. Go take a nap because you're going to need your energy tonight."

Brittany couldn't imagine the pain her sister was experiencing. She loved Macy more than anyone in the entire world, but she wasn't her child. Clint and her sister had built a loving home, something Brittany wanted to achieve with Ryan. Speaking of her fiancé, where was he? She pulled out her phone and saw she'd missed a few texts. Clint was driving around the island, going door to door, asking if anyone had seen Macy. Susan and Elaina were doing the same in Parker's favorite haunts in downtown Charleston. Finding her out in the open was a long shot, but not impossible. Their family needed to feel useful. She understood that sentiment completely. Strangely, there were no texts from Ryan. She shrugged it off, assuming he'd gone off to look for her on his own.

After answering her family's texts, she sent Paulene a message to explain their last-minute request. When Paulene agreed to help, Brittany breathed a sigh of relief. Putting away her phone, she remembered they also needed Granny Mason to be there. But how could she get her attention? Not for the first time, Brittany wished for the ability to text someone who'd crossed over to the Other Side. "Granny?" she called out. "We need you to help us tonight. You were there the first time around. We want Nancy to be with us, too. Can you guys hear me?" There was no response. Walking through the house, she brainstormed other ways to reach her. In the living room, she picked up a family photo album, which flipped open to a page filled with Granny and Nancy's photos at the cottage and the beach when they were younger. She laughed at the sight of them wearing Halloween costumes; Nancy dressed as a clown and Granny as a butterfly. "You've been so lucky to have each other," she whispered.

In her subconscious, she heard, "Almost as lucky as you and your sisters, right?" A gentle breeze pulled her attention to the sofa where Granny Mason and Nancy were sitting.

"Y'all heard me! Thank God! Everything's coming together, so it looks like tonight's the night."

Nancy turned to Granny Mason. "How can we make him suffer extra this time?" Nancy's lips curled into a devilish grin, and she tapped her fingertips together as if she were plotting a scheme.

Brittany shook her head. "Blake doesn't want revenge. She just wants us to focus on Macy. But for the record, I'd like it to hurt extra bad as he's incinerated tonight."

Nancy snapped her fingers and said, "Darn," but the twinkle in her eye told Brittany she had something up her sleeves.

"Be careful, Nan," Granny Mason said. "As much as I'd like to punish Parker, he has our little one. We can't risk her getting caught in the crossfire. I know that's the last thing you'd want to happen."

Nancy folded her hands on her lap and stared at them in defeat. "He's certainly made a fine mess of things. Poor Blake and Clint, and well, I wouldn't be in *this* state if it weren't for him. Wasn't that enough? Did he have to take Macy?"

Granny put her finger to her lips. "Calm down, Nan. He

isn't worth the trouble. We'll take care of everything tonight. Now, let Brittany rest for a bit. You've forgotten how exhausting it is to be alive, let alone dealing with all this evil spirit nonsense."

Nancy patted Brittany's shoulder. "That's a good point. Hon, why don't you go rest for a spell. We'll be right here when you need us."

Brittany said goodbye and ran to the kitchen, where she rummaged through drawers and found the candles they had used five years prior. *Thank goodness Blake is a hoarder and can't bear to throw away anything.* She had the candles and the now blank piece of paper Blake had used for her letter to Parker. Something essential was missing, but what? The night of the fateful ceremony played through her mind. Blake had needed a hand mirror to see if Parker was standing behind her. Brittany shivered. That was a memory that she had hoped she wouldn't need to uncover.

Chapter 11

After her nap, Brittany walked into the kitchen to cook dinner for their family. Frying shrimp and breading okra, she recalled the summers after Blake and Elaina had gone to college. They couldn't visit the island as often. Brittany had Granny Mason to herself for the first time in her life and cherished every minute, especially when they'd cooked Lowcountry food together.

Ryan walked up and lay his head on her shoulder. "Mmm. That smells good. It's nice having a few minutes with you. We've not talked much since I first got here. I didn't realize I'd be at the hospital quite so much, but enough of that. My residency will still end in September, and we can figure out the future then. We're here together right now. Are you ready for tonight?"

"I think so. It's hard to say. We thought we'd done everything right five years ago. At least now, we'll have Granny with us for the whole thing."

He stared at her. "It's hard getting used to your family's, um, quirks. I love them and all, but you have to admit this whole scenario isn't normal."

Brittany scooped the food out of the oil in silence and placed it on a paper-towel covered plate to drain. "No. It's not, but remember, you're the one who randomly showed up here. I wouldn't have asked you to come during such a weird time."

"Hey. Don't be pissed. I didn't mean to offend you. I'm just saying I'd never heard anyone talk about real-life ghosts until you and I spoke about it. After everything your family went through last time, Clint explained what he had learned and warned me I might see a spirit—especially if you were in danger. When you fall in love with someone, they share their powers with you. He said he feels like that's even the whole purpose of the gift—to help your family protect each other." He paused, fidgeting with the buttons on his shirt. "I would never discredit what you guys have experienced. Obviously, Macy has disappeared. I'm so worried about her, just like the rest of the family."

Brittany's chest tightened. "Sorry to be so on edge. This is the hardest thing I've ever experienced, and I still feel responsible for the kidnapping. I was supposed to be caring for her. I let my guard down for twenty minutes. And he took her. I won't be able to forgive myself if we're not able to get her back. I don't think Blake or Clint will, either, and I couldn't blame them."

As she walked outside, a light breeze chilled the air. Brittany's teeth chattered, and she rubbed her arms. "I guess I should have grabbed a jacket." She looked up at Ryan. They'd been together since high school. Their relationship had withstood long-distance dating throughout college and Ryan's time in Seattle. "Thank you for transferring here. I've loved having you around, even though we've not had as much time together as we'd like."

He pursed his lips. "This is where I needed to be."

Fighting back the tears, Brittany kissed his cheek. "That is so amazingly sweet. I love you."

"I love you, too. And I'm not going anywhere."

After dinner, the Nelson women gathered in the upstairs den, waiting for the ceremony to begin. The solemn mood of the room was unsettling. Blake fidgeted with her hands, and Susan jumped at every little sound—the pipes clanking and the ice maker shooting ice cubes into the tray.

"Okay, you guys. We can't sit here anxiously waiting until midnight," Brittany said, not able to take the suspense any longer herself. "The last time we dealt with Parker, we watched old family movies. It helped take our minds off everything back then. It's worth a shot again." She got up and started the video from her sixteenth birthday.

"Look how cute you two were!" Susan exclaimed, holding her heart. Both Brittany and Ryan had braces and glasses at this point in their awkward teenage existence. It was something they had bonded over immediately.

"Yup. We were such nerds, but at least we were nerds for each other, too." Brittany smiled, momentarily forgetting the reason for their gathering until Susan signed that someone was at the door. She jumped to her feet. "That must be Paulene."

She ran down the steps to the front door, opening it to see the aging tall and lean woman wearing her typical head-to-toe flowing black chiffon outfit. The only color came from the rainbow-hued stones in her intricately designed rings that covered each finger. She'd pulled her hair into a tight bun. Brittany tried not to stare at her wardrobe choice. "You can head upstairs. Everyone else is in the den. I'll be up in just a sec."

Paulene gave a slight nod and began climbing the steps. The woman's bangle bracelets jostled as she walked. She might be quite the sight to behold, but they were lucky to have her expertise and support. Brittany pulled a pitcher of tea out of the fridge and grabbed enough glasses for everyone. They all needed to hydrate before the evening's— *gulp*—main event. Walking into the den, she had to stifle a giggle. It was easy to see her mom and sisters were having the same reaction to Paulene's get-up. But she pushed it out of her mind as she poured a glass of tea for everyone. "Hey, guys, drink up. We need to be on our A-game tonight."

On that note, Granny Mason and Nancy appeared in the den. "Yep. We're ready to kick that sorry son of a ..." Nancy said, with her arms folded across her chest. Brittany motioned for her to drop the sass, pointing her head toward Blake. Nancy cleared her throat. "I mean, we're ready when you need us." Brittany mouthed, "Thank you."

Nancy nodded, sitting down next to Blake. "I've missed you, hon. I'm so glad to see you. I can't wait to see my Macy again."

Tears streamed down Blake's face. "I know," she whispered. "Poor Macy. She's so innocent and trusting. He'd better not hurt my baby." Nancy wrapped her arms around Blake, squeezing her.

Brittany bit her lip. Tonight had to go well. They'd undo the cleansing ceremony and redo it, going to extra lengths to make sure it worked this time around. But they'd forgotten one crucial detail. "We forgot about needing a life-changing event to close the door and send Parker on his way!"

Granny Mason tapped her foot. "We just need that boy to marry you." *Geez, Granny, just blurt it right out!* Brittany stifled a laugh and looked over at Ryan, who gawked at her.

"Um...I'm right here."

Brittany put her hands on her hips. "Hush." *Well, it wasn't the worst idea.* "Give me five minutes. I'll go talk to him." She pulled him aside to the front of the house for some privacy. "Hey, I know this is sudden, but how do you feel about getting married tomorrow? It's the only way we'll make sure we send Parker back where he belongs. That's why Clint and Blake had to get married the day after the last cleansing ceremony."

Ryan's eyes widened. "Whoa. That's a lot to throw at a man out of the blue. Let's talk about this a little."

Brittany exhaled. "I'm sorry. I guess that wasn't a very romantic proposal." She put her head in her hands, and her heart ached. What if the love of her life didn't want to marry her anymore? Wouldn't that take the cake? It wasn't the solution she wanted, but maybe she could find someone else to marry her for the day, just so her family could go ahead with finalizing the cleansing ceremony. Clint probably had a single friend who would help them save Macy's life. *God, what has my life come to?*

Ryan pulled her hands away from her face and pulled her in close. "Of course, I'm ready to marry you, and I don't care when or where. Your grandmother just took me by surprise. I'll call my parents to see if they can drive up from Knoxville tomorrow." *Thank God!* She was grateful he'd heard and accepted what Granny Mason had said. Any other man would have run for the hills at the mention of supernatural beings, but not Ryan. He'd stayed by her side for every strange, frightening moment in their relationship.

Jumping up into his arms, she kissed him on the cheek. "You don't know how happy that makes me. I was trying to think of someone, anyone, who would marry me tomorrow, just so this Parker would go away."

"Please don't marry anyone else. I want to be with you more than anything in the world. That's why I'm here right now, and that's why I'll be with you for the rest of our lives."

Chapter 12

Brittany shared her wedding plans with her family against a backdrop of their childhood home movies flickering across the screen and tugging at Brittany's heartstrings.

"I'm so excited for you, sweetheart!" Susan wrapped her arms around Brittany. The hug warmed her heart at such a dark and frightening point in their lives. On one hand, they had the excitement of a wedding, but who could enjoy that knowing that Macy was still missing? The Nelson sisters would find a way through this bump, *or more like a dead skunk*, in the road. They'd always been close and stood with each other through every heartbreak and success. And thanks to Parker, now they could say they'd had each other's back during every haunting. What other family could say that? It had to be an oddity, to say the very least.

At eleven o'clock, the women gathered their supplies and walked outside to the garden. Scowling, Blake rewrote her note to Parker from memory. "I can't believe we have to do this. Once was enough."

Brittany cringed. "I know. I feel sick about it, but we don't have a choice." Digging up the dogwood tree's roots, she moved it aside as much as she could. *Damn, that S.O.B. is heavy.* Wiping sweat from her brow, Brittany unearthed the wooden box and handed it to her sister.

"Ugh…here goes." Blake opened the box and placed the letter inside. "Fingers crossed."

Nancy scurried outside, "One of y'all grab that big bag of salt out of the cupboard and follow me. We're gonna pour a ring of protection around us, so he can't snatch one of you like he did last time." Brittany shivered, remembering how Parker had hidden Susan from them. Luckily, she'd returned unscathed at the end of the ceremony, but it had been frightening, not knowing where she was.

Forming a circle around the tree, each woman took a candle from Blake and used hers to light their own. Brittany looked into their eyes. Few families had been through as many harrowing events as theirs. It had brought them closer, shaping their hearts in such a way that they could feel each other's emotions without saying a word. As Nancy and Paulene sprinkled a trail of salt around them, Brittany could feel the warmth and love that Nancy's soul exuded. Nancy may not be alive, but her compassion and wisdom had lived on after her death. Even Paulene, who the Nelson sisters hadn't met until Parker's first haunting, had a special connection and bond with them. God had blessed their family with an incredible amount of love.

Brittany looked at her grandmother and shrugged. "What's next?"

"We have to burn the tree down to the roots, taking the letter with it."

Brittany gulped. Fires could do unrepairable damage within minutes. Other than becoming a mother, dying in a fire was her biggest fear. Shaking, she moved closer to the tree and dropped a lit match at its base. Holding her breath, she watched as the flames twisted up the trunk of the tree and shot into the air. She twisted her hands and exhaled. *One step closer.*

"Everyone repeat after me. 'Spirit, we sent you home, but you've gone astray. Reveal yourself to us so we may forever send you away.'"

Shaking, Brittany watched the women repeat Granny Mason's words as she did the same. Would Parker show his face? Would Macy be with him? Could they banish him forever? It had to work; Macy didn't deserve to be at the will of a demented spirit.

Granny Mason pointed to Blake. "Hold up the hand mirror. Do you see him?"

Blake closed her eyes and pulled the mirror in front of her face, opening one eye at a time. Her mouth widened, and she collapsed, sending broken mirror shards across the grass.

"What happened? Did anyone else see? Is she okay?" Brittany blurted out as she ran to her sister to wake her. Everyone shook their heads as they came to help.

After a couple of minutes, Blake came to crying. "Macy was with him, looking back at me in the mirror. What does that mean?"

Out of the corner of Brittany's eye, she saw Parker strut up to the edge of the salt. "You guys, don't look now, but we've got company!"

"Well, hello, there, ladies. Thanks ever so much for undoing that shameful ceremony. I appreciate the freedom after all this time."

"What do you mean?" Brittany asked. "You've been free all along."

He held his head high, chuckling. "Come on out, Maggie. I see our scheme worked." A carbon copy of Parker appeared beside him. He rubbed his chin and looked around at the Nelson family. *Oh, my God! How could they have forgotten about Parker's twin sister, Maggie?* She'd died about a year before Parker. Brittany had seen framed pictures of her at Parker's parents' house when she'd visited with Blake and remembered how much they looked alike. Her short hair and athletic build were identical to Parker's. Their matching baseball caps hid any small cosmetic differences.

"Well, since I died, my good ol' sis kept in touch with me through the spiritual network, think of it as texting for ghosts, and we've been a-plotting! Not only is our likeness uncanny, but she can mimic my voice to a 'T.' Long story short, Maggie tricked you guys into thinking she was me. She kidnapped Macy. We knew you'd reverse the errors you made five years ago. But I didn't think it would take you so long to try. It's almost as if you don't care about finding your little one."

A fire raged in Brittany's stomach. Damn it, Parker and Maggie had outsmarted them, staying two steps ahead at every turn. How could the Nelson sisters reclaim an advantage? There had to be a way to trick the Suttons and regain some ground in getting Macy back to safety.

Parker walked over to Blake, who shook her balled fists at him. "How adorable. You think you're going to threaten me. Don't waste your energy. You're looking sort of pale like you've seen a ghost or something."

Blake pulled herself up. "Bring Macy here, now!" she demanded.

"What's in it for me? Are you gonna give up the ghost and be with me? I'll be happy to arrange your death."

Blake opened her mouth to respond, but Brittany pushed herself in front of her sister. "You can have me instead. I'll do whatever you want, but you have to leave our family alone forever. If you don't, Granny will see that you and Maggie suffer."

"No! Don't do this, Britt!" Blake screamed. "Nancy says something is wrong—he's too powerful—we'll find another way to get Macy back."

Blake had planned the cleansing ceremony with Granny's help last time. They were the most likely to find a solution again.

Brittany freed herself from her sister's grasp. "It's okay. This whole ordeal is my fault. I should pay for my mistakes." She stepped outside the circle, cringing as she grabbed Parker's hand.

Something was happening to her body. Starting with her toes, each inch of her body pulled on the next, almost as if she were melting. When the sensation stopped, she was no longer standing near her family. But, where were they? The glow of the moonlight illuminated Parker's wild-eyed

73

expression. "Don't look down." He laughed.

Brittany wished she'd obeyed this command, but she did not. Somehow, they were flying over the tumultuous Atlantic Ocean, hugging the coastline as the waves crashed against the shore. *Oh, God!* She squeezed her eyes closed for a moment, but the sharp wind told her they were still airborne.

Parker snorted. "Don't even think of screaming, or I'll drop you, and you'll splatter like a bug."

Even if she had screamed, it was dark; no one would have seen her or been able to help. She would have drifted away into the depths of the ocean, never found again. *This is not how I expected the evening to go.* She held her breath for a moment, trying to forget she was soaring 1,000 feet over the Lowcountry. Nothing in Granny's book had prepared her for anything like this. Upon exhaling, she asked, "Where are you taking me?"

"You'll see soon enough." She closed her eyes for the rest of the journey, not opening them until her feet hit solid ground. *Thank the Lord! I wish I could kiss the ground right now!*

Parker dug his fist into her back and prodded her to start walking. The darkness didn't allow her to see much, but they were in a secluded area, surrounded by trees and water. A small unwelcoming cabin was less than a quarter of a mile ahead. Its foundation was crumbling; the paint was peeling, and the shutters looked like they had come halfway unhinged many years ago. Was Macy inside? Was Maggie? She shuddered. How had Parker's sister fooled them so well?

Hopeful of finding her niece, she opened the cabin door, but there wasn't anyone inside the shack other than a few spiders. She walked to the bathroom to make sure Macy wasn't in there, but she thanked God for her niece's absence when she saw the room. Broken glass covered the floor, and a mouse squeaked as it jumped into the register vent. *Ick.*

"Where's Macy?" Brittany asked.

Parker shrugged. "You didn't actually think I'd let you be

near her yet, did you? Maggie is with her…somewhere else. You're gonna have to earn my trust by proving you aren't up to something."

She should have known it wouldn't be that easy. *Please, God, let my family figure out how to send these deranged twins back where they belong and free Macy and me. If you can only save one of us, save her. Amen.*

"What are you daydreaming about?" Parker sneered. "You're mine now, and I have plans for us to torment your sister."

"I only came with you if you let Macy go home and left my family alone. That was the deal. If you won't hold up your end of the bargain, I may as well leave." She walked to the door, but the knob wouldn't turn.

Parker appeared next to her. "You've forgotten who's in charge here. Let me remind you; it's me. If you try to run, I'll go back to the cottage and set fire to the whole place. That's right, I know about your little phobia. Your whole family would go up in flames. Is that what you want?"

She got in his face. "You wouldn't dare. You know Nancy and Granny would hunt your dead ass down and deliver you to the devil himself if that's what it takes. Anyway, you enjoy tormenting Blake way too much. You might kill me, but you wouldn't take a chance that you might kill her. Here's how this is going to go down. You're going to tell your sister to take Macy home. Then, you'll take me there, so I can make sure she's safe."

"Hmm. I'd forgotten how feisty you are, but now I remember, you're the family spitfire. That could come in handy," Parker said, rubbing his chin. "Fine. We'll do this your way." He held out his hand. Brittany shivered as she took it. The same bubbling, melting sensation overtook her body. Looking down, she saw they were in the air, hugging the coastline, once again. "You're not afraid of heights, are ya?" He laughed.

"Nope. I'm not. Just take me to Macy," she demanded.

Chapter 13

Several minutes later, she was standing in her grandmother's garden, face-to-face with Maggie. "OK, where is she? And if you did anything to hurt her, you sick…"

Maggie twisted her mouth, interrupting. "Don't talk to me that way. I'm the one with the power right now. You will treat me with respect or else…"

Macy popped out from behind Maggie, jumping up and down. "Auntie Britt! So happy to see you. Love you!" Brittany's heart swelled—her niece was safe. That's all that mattered in the big scheme of things. *Thank you, God, for watching over our adorable little one.* She scooped up Macy, kissed her forehead and began walking her into the cottage.

Maggie blinked. "We're following you."

"I didn't expect anything different," Brittany said through her teeth, rolling her eyes. She rang the doorbell.

Blake came to the door, freezing in place. "Britt! You have Macy! How? Where was she?" Blake's crestfallen expression told Brittany she'd just noticed Parker and Maggie. "What do they want?" she asked, pointing at them.

Maggie made a crude gesture, but Parker motioned for her to let it go.

Fighting back the tears, Brittany set Macy down. "Go inside and go to bed right now. Don't talk to your friends anymore. And I mean never. Do you understand?" Macy nodded and ran inside. Brittany gave her niece a minute to get out of earshot before she continued. "I made a deal with Parker," Brittany said. "I'm making him uphold his part of the agreement—to return Macy safe and sound, but he's going to take me."

Blake began signing. "Please don't go. We'll fight them right now however we can, even if it's just a short-term plan. We can get them off our backs while we figure out something more permanent."

Brittany shook her head. "A deal is a deal. I'll go for now. If you guys figure out a way around it, so be it. If not…" She swallowed.

"Don't give up! I'm so sorry this is happening. Granny, Nancy and I are trying to end this. For now, take this necklace." Blake removed the gold chain from her neck and placed it on Brittany, hooking the clasp.

The simple nautical knot pendant shimmered a brilliant gold. "A magical amulet?" She ran her fingers over its smooth texture.

Blake laughed. "No, it has a GPS tracker built into it. After everything we went through last time, Clint bought it from one of his private investigator buddies. Parker will expect magic, so hopefully, this goes under his radar. We'll find you when we're able to end this. I love you, sis." Tears spilled out of Blake's eyes.

"What in the hell is that?" Parker asked, grabbing the necklace out of Brittany's hands and examining it. He gripped it with both hands as if to break it.

"No, Parker!" Brittany screamed. "That's a family heirloom, and it means a lot to me. This might be the last time I see my sister. Can't I keep this one memento?"

Parker's mouth widened into an evil grin. "I suppose that's harmless. I don't see any crosses on *this* one. You know the old saying about fooling someone once or twice. Well, this would be the third time, and that ain't gonna happen, ladies." He turned to Brittany. "Say your goodbyes. It's time for us to go home."

She looked at Blake and signed, "Please tell everyone I

love them." Would she ever get to see her family again? Did Parker plan to kill her? Better me than Macy. Brittany held back tears as she waved goodbye to her sister, the cottage and her life as she knew it.

"Parker, don't take her! She hasn't done anything to you," Blake cried, reaching out for Brittany, who wished she could comfort her sister.

Brittany noticed Ryan sneaking in from the other room. He turned to her and signed. "How are we going to take them down?"

"I'm still working on it, but I'll fill you in soon."

"I've been doing some paranormal research…Let me try this." Ryan stepped into Parker and Maggie's view. "I command you to depart from here!" He held up a small Bible, like most hotels kept in their rooms. "Leave in the name of all that is holy!"

Parker didn't so much as look in his direction before grabbing Brittany's hand and taking flight. The melting sensation was over much faster this time. Even though the wind chilled her skin, an unexpected eerie peacefulness overcame her as she took in the view of the moonlit tidal creeks and their glowing spartina grass.

When they landed, she ran for the cabin. Earlier that morning, she wouldn't have expected ever to be happy to see this ramshackle place, but there was a fireplace, and she planned to use it. There was no telling how long it had been since someone had built a fire in the hearth. She shivered. Hopefully, she wouldn't burn the whole place down. She rubbed her arms. "Parker, I swear I'm not trying to run away. I just need some firewood. It is freezing, and I don't have a coat."

"I thought you were afraid of fire." He stared at her. "Very well. Go ahead, but if you take off, I'll hunt you down and make you regret it."

Ignoring his arrogant comment, she grabbed all the loose limbs she could find, stacking them on the dilapidated front porch. Soon, she'd gathered kindling enough to get through the night and walked inside. She scanned the room for matches or a lighter. Finally, her eyes landed on a jar filled with matchbooks on the kitchen counter. Brittany shuddered, not looking forward to building a fire, but she'd freeze otherwise. The business name on the matchbook, Sweetgrass Island Charters, caught her eye. Was she on Sweetgrass Island? The remote island would make the perfect place to hide or kill someone you'd kidnapped. It was a morbid thought, but unfortunately, a true one. The metallic gold phone number on the matchbook was slightly scratched. She couldn't quite make out the last two digits, not that she had her phone with her. Maybe there was an old landline lying around somewhere. She'd have to look tomorrow.

As the flames grew, so did her comfort, if you could call it that. This situation was far from ideal, but her family was concocting a plan to rescue her and send the evil Sutton twins to their final resting place. She couldn't stop yawning. Assessing the room, she found a faded denim quilt that appeared less filthy than other things in the cabin. The worn blue sofa in the corner would serve as a decent enough bed. Brittany shivered. *Hopefully, no critters find their way to me in the middle of the night.*

Lying down, she tossed and turned. The couch was far from comfortable, with its lumpy and torn cushions, but it would have to do. She drifted off after a short time. In her dreams, she was on the beach, building a sandcastle with Macy. Out of nowhere, Granny Mason appeared. "Hey, Britt, I'm not sure how long I'll have here. On Saturday, you've got to convince Parker to bring you to the cottage. We have a plan based on the upcoming eclipse, so it has to be Saturday. Clint could track that necklace; he will come for you if something happens, but we stand a stronger chance of succeeding this time if you can hang on a couple more days. I know this is hard. But if he thinks you're on his side, he's more likely to leave everyone alone until we can get this situation under control. I'll be right here with you the whole time if you need me. I promise." Granny blew her a kiss and faded into nothingness.

Chapter 14

Brittany snapped back into consciousness as Parker shook her shoulder, demanding, "Who were you talking to?" He began pacing the rutted wooden floors, the red-glowing embers illuminating his face and creating a menacing background. He mouthed something Brittany couldn't quite make out, cutting his eyes back and forth.

She stared at him, pursing her lips. "No one. I must have been talking in my sleep."

"Well, good. I was afraid that busy body neighbor across the way was over here trying to stir up trouble with me again. Don't even think about trying to find their house. You can trust them about as much as you do me."

Brittany turned with her back to Parker and curled up with the tattered quilt. She didn't relish the idea of sleeping with Parker around, but it wouldn't be the first time. Holding onto her wakefulness as long as possible, she tried to plan the next few days. How could she stay safe and avoid Parker? Could she give him a spoonful of his own medicine and send him on a wild goose chase? Slipping back into sleep, she thought about her grandmother, who wove herself into her dreams once again.

"How can I get rid of him while we're waiting for the eclipse?" Brittany asked. "Is there somewhere we can send him or something we can do?"

Granny Mason nodded. "I'll be here in the morning. Go along with whatever I say, and I'll take care of the rest."

Even while sleeping, Brittany's mind churned. After

81

hours of being on the cusp of waking, she finally pulled herself off the couch and stretched. The loose springs and worn cushions hadn't done her any favors. Desperate for water, Brittany walked to the kitchen. She was afraid of what creepy crawlies might live there, but hydration was a necessity. As she reached for the refrigerator door, Parker appeared in front of her. "What are you doing?" he asked.

"I need something to drink and some food."

Parker rolled his eyes. "I don't miss being hungry. My dad still comes here to fish sometimes. You should be able to get water out of the tap. Dig through the pantry if you want."

She stood there, frozen in her tracks, and narrowed her eyes. Why would he offer to help her?

"Well, I don't want you to die of starvation or dehydration. Where's the fun in that?" He sneered. "No. I've got a complex game plan ready for us. After you help me take care of Blake."

Brittany ignored him and walked outside with him on her heels. "Why are you following me? I know where I am, and I can't escape without a boat. You may as well let me be."

He stormed off, back into the house, slamming the door even though he could have walked through without even turning the doorknob.

Thank goodness. Breathing in the salty marsh air and taking in the water view, she almost forgot her current circumstances. She lay back and closed her eyes.

In her semi-conscious state, Granny Mason came to her. "Child, now's the time. I need to talk to you. Blake, Clint and Nancy are leaving for Wilmington right now." She cleared her throat and raised her already booming voice. "They've found something sure to distract Parker and Maggie for at least a little while."

Her grandmother stood still. "Speaking of the devil, they're coming right now. I'll be back after they leave."

Maggie and Parker appeared on the porch, and Maggie

turned to Brittany. "You'd better not go anywhere while we're gone. I know how to find you."

"Again, I don't have a boat. How am I going to leave?"

Maggie stomped her foot on a splintered board and vanished along with Parker. Brittany threw her hands in the air to celebrate. "That worked almost too well. Hopefully, they'll spend some quality time alone."

"Amen to that." Granny Mason wrapped her arm around her. "I'm happy they fell for it. Nancy, Blake and Clint have quite the shenanigans planned for them. Let's just say they're going on a scavenger hunt that will lead him up the East Coast for the better part of a day."

Brittany smirked while imagining Parker and Maggie finding clues, trying to unravel the mystery of how her family was going to send them away. "So, you guys have a plan, right?"

"Of course, we do! Silly goose!" Granny smiled, sitting down. "We're going to get 'em good. I don't want to go into details in case they're spying on us. Don't worry. We'll make sure you're safe."

"I'm not worried about myself. I just want everyone else to be okay. Am I crazy to think that Parker is stronger now that Maggie is here? I mean, how did he fly, carrying me? You and Nancy aren't able to do that, are you?"

Granny shook her head. "Parker and Maggie feed off each other's abilities. They were both stronger than your average spirit before reuniting, but because they share the bond of twins, they're *almost* unstoppable. In life, Nancy and I learned how to harness our abilities to send spirits packing, and we can guide you girls during your journey, but I'm afraid it's gonna take the living to get rid of the dead. Just remember that there's safety in numbers. I know y'all always have each other's backs, so no worries there."

So, that's why Parker had more physical powers than previously. It was more than frightening to consider everything he'd done with these gifts. Pushing the thought out of her mind, she took a deep breath. "How is Ryan handling all of this?"

Granny Mason squeezed her hand. "Honey, I don't think Blake has called to let him know what's going on with you. She probably didn't want to scare him, but we are going to need him to fly here as soon as possible so you two can get hitched this weekend, sealing the door to the Other Side with this whole cleansing ceremony mess. I know it's not the wedding you imagined, but all that matters is you've got a good one."

Brittany cocked her head and raised an eyebrow. "Wait, what are you talking about? Ryan's been at the cottage since the day Macy disappeared."

Granny Mason shook her head. "Honey, we've not seen him since before your graduation. We didn't want to say anything to you when he didn't show up to support you that day because we know he's been busy, but we thought it was odd that he didn't come."

"He was there! He posed for pictures with us and everything." Brittany's chest heaved. Perhaps her grandmother's spirit didn't have a great memory? She couldn't have imagined him being there, could she?

"No, honey. Your mom commented on how sad it was that he couldn't be in your graduation pictures. She was disappointed he didn't come."

"Look, Granny, I swear to you he was there. He spent the night with me at my apartment. I won't forget that night anytime soon." Brittany blushed. *I never thought I'd talk about my sex life to my grandmother.*

"I see what you're saying, but I'm telling you none of us have seen him this whole time. I wonder…"

Brittany's head fell as she considered the unthinkable. "Does that mean—" She paused. He couldn't be dead. If he were, most of her family would have seen him due either to being dead themselves or having the blessing.

What is going on? Tears splashed her shoulders as she shook her head furiously.

Granny Mason grimaced. "He can't be dead. Otherwise, we'd see him for sure. Don't fret about this, child. I'll look into it from the otherworldly perspective, and I'll have Clint try to track him down in his human form. I'm sure there's a logical explanation. If something were wrong with him, I would have expected you to get a phone call from his family or the authorities by now."

Brittany's chest tightened, and her stomach churned. "There's a voicemail on my phone that didn't transcribe properly. I was going to ask Mom to listen to it, but then Macy went missing. Please go back to the cottage now and see if someone can listen to the message for me. Blake knows my passcode. I have to know he's okay. I won't be able to rest until I'm sure of it."

Her grandmother nodded. "I'll be right back." She blew her a kiss before she disappeared.

Chapter 15

The worn rug's fibers scratched the soles of Brittany's feet as she shifted her weight from one foot to the next. *Ugh, Granny, hurry back!* What could take so long? Had her grandmother gotten bad news? Was she trying to figure out how to deliver it without totally shattering Brittany's world?

Her knees buckled underneath her, and she hit the floor. Brittany rolled onto her back, and memories flooded her mind. The day they'd met was her favorite. While searching for her Biology classroom on her first day of high school, he had fallen down the staircase, landing at her feet. She'd offered him her hand, but as he stood, undamaged except for his ego, she fell on top of him. They'd laughed until a teacher came to intervene, separating them and threatening detention if they didn't get to class right away. As fate had it, the teacher couldn't keep them apart for long. Brittany grinned when he followed her into the classroom. The intensity of how he'd studied her had both intrigued and unnerved her. When the bell rang, he handed her a note with his phone number and name. They'd fallen in love hard and fast, and to this day, their bond inspired her existence in every sense.

A breeze swirled around Brittany, her hair flying into her face. An iridescent film filled the air, and Granny Mason appeared.

Brittany jumped to her feet, signing, "What did you find out? Where is Ryan? Is he okay?" She twisted her hands.

"Sit down, child—" Granny Mason paused. "There were

two voicemails. One from a doctor at a hospital in Atlanta and another from his mom, which she left yesterday morning."

"What happened? Just tell me." Brittany folded her trembling hands on her lap to steady them. *This would not be good news.*

"He just came out of a coma two days ago. Some kids found Ryan lying unconscious outside the Midtown metro station in Atlanta. He didn't have a wallet or ID on him, but luckily, one of his medical school friends was on rotation. She tracked down his parents, and they're with him now." Her grandmother bit her lip.

Brittany rubbed her eyes and coughed. Her hands trembling, she signed, "Do they think he's okay now?"

Granny Mason placed her hand on Brittany's face and pulled away. "I wish I knew, sweetie. All we can do is pray for him. Blake has been trying to reach his mom to find out more; I just wanted to come back and let you know he's...alive."

"How did he come to my graduation and to the island? How did we make love, all while he's in a coma? Is that why no one else can see him? But why can I see him and even feel his touch? I'm going out of my mind trying to figure out what in the world is happening to me." She sobbed, placing her head into her hands.

Granny Mason sat down and stroked Brittany's hair. "When we were young, Paulene's brother was injured while fighting in the war. While he was unconscious, his, um, *essence* came to visit her, had dinner with their family and even helped around the farm. She thought he'd come back for good, but later that month, his mother received a telegram saying he'd died in the hospital that very week. It turns out Paulene was the only one who saw her brother during his visit. Over the years, she's collected similar stories from other families. While someone is unconscious, only one person can see and communicate with them. And that person must have the blessing. I'll go talk to her now to see if she has any ideas how to help him."

Brittany sighed as her grandmother vanished into a silvery mist. Just the thought of talking to and making love to Ryan's essence made her stomach churn. This wasn't normal, not even in her bizarre ghost-seeing family. What else would the Nelson sisters have to endure?

After a couple of minutes, the stress took its toll, zapping every ounce of energy out of her body. She fell back onto the couch, crying herself to sleep. Dreams of Maggie and Parker torturing Macy and Blake swirled through her mind. In the last dream, Ryan burst through the door, opening a jewel-covered box that sucked the Sinister Suttons' spirits into its depths. What did that mean?

In what seemed like mere minutes later, she woke in a sweat, jumping when she saw her grandmother seated beside her. "You scared me to death! Did you sit there staring at me the whole time?" Brittany pulled the threadbare quilt around her shoulders and fought the urge to shiver.

"Calm down, sweetheart. I come bearing some good news. Blake talked to Ryan's mom. He's doing much, much better."

Brittany fist pumped. "Thank God! I've never been more relieved. I need to see him or at least talk to him through a video chat. There are so many things I want to say to him. I should be there for him. That's it. I'm busting out of here and go back to Atlanta. That's where I should be right now." She pushed her way past her grandmother and walked outside.

Granny Mason stepped in front of her and held up her hand. "Honey, you're going to have to be patient. The truth of the matter is we don't have a boat here for you yet. Anyway, if you leave, you risk Maggie and Parker following you and hurting Ryan again."

"Wait, do you think they had something to do with Ryan getting hurt in Atlanta?"

The horizon seemed to spin before her. Grabbing the

porch railing, she looked up at her grandmother.

Granny Mason nodded. "Don't you?"

"I guess I hadn't considered the possibility, but it makes complete sense." Brittany clenched her fists. "Agh! Of course, they did!"

Her grandmother pursed her lips. "I didn't finish telling you this part. He told the police he didn't see his attacker. The last thing he remembered was stopping at a florist shop before your graduation. Knowing all of this, don't you think Ryan is better off with you being in a different state right now? I know that's a difficult decision to make. You two are so perfect together, but God will bring you back to each other when the time is right. Paulene is going to visit him tomorrow. She's pretty sure that she can help speed up his recovery process."

As usual, Granny Mason had a solution, but that didn't make the situation any less maddening. More than anything, Brittany wanted to lie on her fiancé's chest and tell him everything was going to be okay. Her body ached for his embrace; she longed to talk to him. Their conversations put all others to shame—even a simple exchange brought on an inward glow that Brittany had never experienced with another person.

Suddenly, she realized she hadn't seen Parker or Maggie in hours. Were they still chasing her family's trail of breadcrumbs down the Eastern Seaboard? What could have enticed them to stay on the chase to this point? Not that she wanted them around, but they didn't take the wishes of others into account. It was only a matter of time before they returned. Now was a good time to settle in for a nap and help conserve energy for whatever came next. She covered herself with the quilt and fought off the inevitable nightmares that skirted the edges of her consciousness.

Chapter 16

L ater that day, Granny Mason grabbed Brittany's hand. "I have something to show you. C'mon." As they ran toward the dock, Brittany strained to see what was so urgent.

"What are we looking for exactly?" She shielded her eyes. "I don't see a boat."

"Patience, Britt. Just follow me. Anyway, you've gotta stay here to keep Parker and Maggie preoccupied until we can do the cleansing ceremony again. Don't worry, though, I promise that Nancy and I are keeping an eye on you and the rest of the family."

Brittany nodded, taking in the small windowless outbuilding where her grandmother stood. Tools and landscaping equipment filled the shelves, only lit by sunlight filtering through a crack in the roof. Nothing stood out from her perspective, but her grandmother must have had a good reason to be excited.

"Look what I found!" Granny Mason motioned toward a fishing net, rod and tackle box. "You won't be going hungry anytime soon! Let's go drop this net in and see what we can catch."

Brittany gathered up the net, and as she approached the water, she recalled shrimping and crabbing with her grandmother as a child. The memories brought a smile to her face.

"What are you smiling about?"

"Just remembering hanging out with you when I was a

kid."

"I loved your visits. Teaching you girls how to catch your dinner was quite amusing." Granny winked. "Do you remember the time Blake's fishing line broke, and you and Elaina caught a fish before her? She wouldn't speak to either of you for a couple of days. She was so stubborn."

Brittany laughed. "Was? She still is. Hey, so how long do I need to wait before I check the net? And how are we going to cook whatever we catch? We can build a fire, but I doubt there's a pot or anything in the kitchen."

"I'd leave it there for at least a few hours. I'm one step ahead of you," Granny said, walking behind the cabin. In the clearing stood a tall brick oven, housing a cast iron grill grate. "See, it should be smooth sailing from here, hon. I'm going to the cottage to check in with Blake, but I'll be back in a flash." Brittany waved to her grandmother, who faded away, and returned to the cabin.

Brittany couldn't believe their luck. Once she caught some food, she'd be in great shape. Walking the property's perimeter, she looked for signs of neighbors or even day-trippers, seeking solitude on the quiet island. There wasn't a soul around, which was probably for the best. She didn't need some busybody bothering her while she waited out the clock.

Not having a phone or a watch was unsettling, but it was probably around three or four in the afternoon if she had to guess. Before it got dark and Maggie and Parker returned, she needed to assess what useful items might lie around the cabin. She walked back inside. In the daylight and without her captors' presence, the house took on a less menacing tone. The furnishings were dated and worn, but someone had put a lot of thought into the room's layout and color palette—shades of blue and light beige—just like the ocean. For the first time, she walked past the kitchen, finding herself inside a mudroom.

A leaning bookcase had been propped against one wall, filled with dozens of books. Holding her breath, Brittany slipped her hand in the gap between the white wooden bookcase and the wall. Her fingers ran over a trim board and a divot in the wall. *A door!* Brittany gave the bookcase a push, but it didn't budge. What was preventing it from toppling over? She examined it from top to bottom. A crumpled rug held the base of the bookcase in place. If only she had something to help shift it, even just a few inches. Oddly enough, a metal broom handle had been stashed in the corner as if it were waiting for this moment. She grabbed it and used it to pry the bookcase away from the door. *BINGO.*

What could be worth going to such great lengths to hide? Opening the door, she held her breath. Light from an uncovered window stung her eyes. She shielded them and walked inside the room to see hundreds of books piled up wall to wall. Why hide them? She picked up one, *Sending Spirits Onward.* Another, *Giving up the Ghost: Ending a Haunting,* was lying underneath it. Digging through the stacks, she read dozens of titles around the same themes, written by different authors. Where in the heck did these books come from? A ghost couldn't drive a boat, so how did Parker and Maggie transport these heavy suckers here?

Brittany found a book with a slightly different bent, *Raising Hell—How to Bring A Loved One's Spirit Back.* The book slipped out of her fingers and crashed onto the floor. Maggie had been looking for a means to bring Parker back all this time. *Damn it!* They'd played the Nelson sisters like a fiddle.

Gulping, she picked up the book. The first chapter outlined what to do if someone had banished a spirit by mistake. Sending Parker to his next destination hadn't been an error in Brittany's eyes, but she could see how his sister would have a different point of view, albeit a twisted one. Flipping through the pages for clues to the Sutton twins' thought process, she landed on a section describing how to protect a spirit from being sent back to the Other Side.

In the case of a former lover sending a spirit away, you

must take someone they care about and turn the person against them. When you've been successful, ask your new devotee to kill their loved one.

Brittany shook her head. That wouldn't happen; she'd never kill Blake. But she'd attempt to convince Parker that she would. It was worth trying to get back to the cottage for whatever her family was cooking up. "Granny!" she called out, hoping her grandmother would return before Parker so she could share her plan.

A short time later, Granny Mason finally appeared. "Sorry, sugar. I was helping throw Parker off Nancy's trail, but he's still picking up the clues. I didn't think we'd be able to fool him for this long, but I'm glad he's not here bothering you."

Brittany nodded and handed the book to her grandmother, whose face fell while reading through its pages.

"I think I can trick him into thinking I'm on his side…"

"Are you sure? Your plan could go horribly wrong. Don't take any chances."

"I have to be there to help protect my family," Brittany said. "You should know that feeling better than anyone. Let me help."

Julia Caroline's lips twisted. "I do, but I wish I hadn't passed every single one of my flaws down to you girls. It would devastate me if something happened to any of you."

"Something's been bothering me," Brittany said. "From what we understood, the blessing skipped generations. So why has Macy been cursed with this *gift*?"

"You girls inherited my gifts, just as I had gotten them from my grandmother. Macy inherited her gifts from Clint's mother, Nancy's daughter-in-law. After Clint's parents died, Nancy never brought up his mom's abilities to him. There didn't seem to be a reason at the time, but we've since realized we were wrong to keep it from him. Of course, Macy hasn't fully realized her abilities yet because she hasn't been through a traumatic event. Even this kidnapping seemed like a game of hide and go seek to her. Thank God for that."

Brittany buried her head in her hands. *Poor Macy*.

Chapter 17

The moth-eaten curtains in the house flapped against the open windows. With the sun going down, the breeze made the South Carolina heat almost bearable. Brittany fanned herself with a magazine, Lowcountry Luxury, she'd found among the stack of books and yellowed newspaper clippings in the bedroom. The date across the top of the front cover read June 1988, and the cover image featured a couple dressed in matching gray and white pinstriped business suits. A simple headline read: *Newlyweds leading the way in island luxury.*

Just past their 1980s yuppie aesthetic, there was something familiar about them, especially their fake, plastered-on smiles and glistening green eyes. She flipped through a third of the pages to read the article. In the subhead, she found what she was looking for—Reginald and Deidre, aka Reggie and DeeDee, Sutton. *This article was about Maggie and Parker's parents!* Brittany had met them at various events Blake and Parker had hosted in Knoxville. That's why their photos were familiar. Blake hadn't ever mentioned the Sutton family had ties to the Lowcountry. Did she know? Brittany shivered.

Flipping through the magazine and newspaper clippings, Brittany learned about the Sutton family's twisted history in the Lowcountry. Reggie and DeeDee had met while attending college in Charleston. After graduating, Reggie had become influential in the area and tried to commercialize Isle of Palms in the late 80s. But many longtime residents put up a fight, blocking his attempts through zoning technicalities. When Reggie didn't make headway, he bought some property on Sweetgrass Island under a pseudonym. The young couple built a small but beautiful resort, catering to celebrities who wanted a luxurious but under the radar Lowcountry vacation. The hotel was right on the water's edge with balconies overlooking the Intracoastal Waterway. Brittany's heart sank as she read the next part—on the night of the grand opening, the Suttons shot off fireworks from their yacht to celebrate. Unfortunately, it had been a historically dry summer. Embers from the fireworks landed on the dry sea oats and spread like, well, wildfire. More than 200 people died that night. Some burned in the fire. Others jumped from their balconies into the water but landed on the rocky shoreline. *How frightening and sad!* Tears splashed onto the pages as a silvery mist filled the air, and Granny Mason appeared.

"Granny, do you know anything about all of this?" Brittany held up the clippings.

Her grandmother nodded. "People who visit the island say they have seen the victims' spirits both on land and in the water as if they are part mermaid. The locals started calling them mermaids, even though there aren't any fins or scales on their bodies."

Brittany's jaw gaped. "That's horrible! I feel so bad for those poor people!" She drew a deep breath. "So, is that when Parker's parents moved back to Knoxville?"

Granny Mason frowned. "Yes. They left. No one wanted them around these parts anymore. They'd been responsible for the deaths of too many people's loved ones. Parker's grandpa ended up paying out millions in settlements with the families, but the Suttons are so rich, I doubt they even missed the money."

Brittany gulped. "Have you ever seen the um, mermaids?"

"I have, but I've always tried to avoid them and

Sweetgrass Island. I never wanted to be surrounded by the negative energy. Speaking of which, I think I heard Parker muttering to himself. I'd best be hiding. Don't worry, though. I'll be waiting in the wings in case you need me." She winked at Brittany before fading away to nothingness.

Parker appeared next to the fireplace but slid across the floor, stooping where his mouth was at Brittany's eye level.

"Back up! Just because I read lips doesn't mean I need you to be in my face," she growled at him.

He scooted backward a few steps. "I'm pissed. I don't know what your sister and that dim-witted husband of hers were up to today. Your friend, Nancy, led Maggie and me all around North and South Carolina, getting me all twisted up in knots."

Brittany resisted the urge to laugh, sitting as still as possible.

Parker knocked the magazine off the table but scanned the cover when it hit the floor. "Where didya get that from?"

Brittany shrugged. "It's just an old magazine."

His lips turned up into a snarl. "You found Maggie's room, didn't you? Maggie paid a visit to our mother's cousin, who has the gift, as your family calls it. She collected those books for Maggie. She didn't ask questions about why we wanted them, so we didn't offer any answers. Anyway, I'm guessing you had a little history lesson about my family and this island. My parents shouldn't have kept all of those old newspapers and magazines. Well, it doesn't matter now. Our plans worked out perfectly. Now, we just need to ruin Blake's life completely, right in front of her eyes. If you help me, you'll get to live."

Brittany cleared her mind and numbed her heart. "Sure. Whatever you need me to do, just say the word. I've got so much living ahead of me, I can't die yet."

"I hope I can trust you. It would certainly make everything so much easier!" Parker rubbed his hands together, pacing the room with precise steps.

"So, why have you and Maggie been hanging out here?

Why did you bring me here?"

He turned around and scowled. "Since you've been snooping, you may as well know. This was my grandfather's fishing cabin. My dad loved coming here as a kid, so he went to college in Charleston and lived in the cabin on the weekends. He met my mom in college. They ended up moving into the cabin while they built their dream hotel. When their business didn't work out as planned, they slinked back to Knoxville. My grandpa gave my dad a job at the family law firm, where I worked, too. It was a good thing that hotel burned down. Otherwise, my parents wouldn't have moved back home, and I wouldn't have met my lovely Blake. And that's a concept I don't even want to entertain. I brought you here because it's remote, and unless you've built a boat or sprouted wings while I've been gone, you're not going anywhere without me."

Brittany's fingernails dug into her palms. Why did Parker have to meet Blake? He'd brought an incredible amount of pain into their family members' lives. How could anyone, even Parker, talk about the innocent lives lost in the hotel fire in such a nonchalant way? Brittany excused herself, saying she needed to lie down. Tears stung her eyes, but she couldn't free them in front of Parker. *Stay strong for Blake. For Macy. For your family.*

Chapter 18

T he scent of burning firewood wafted into the cabin, waking Brittany the next morning. She ran outside to find the source of the smoke and saw her grandmother hunched over the brick oven, cooking. "Good morning, Darlin'. I didn't know for sure if I'd be able to start the stove, but it looks like I've still got it." She winked. "I waited until Parker and Maggie left the island to show my face. Ryan sends his love. He overnighted this to you." She handed Brittany a silver envelope and winked. "Go ahead and read it."

Brittany sat down on a wrought-iron chair that had seen better days and unfolded the simple white card. The front had a single royal-blue bird on it. The interior featured the word *love* embossed in silver text and a short-handwritten note—*Britt, I know you're worried about me, but don't be. You have enough on your plate. You're the bravest, most selfless person I've ever met. The good news is I'm doing a lot better now. The doctor told me to take it easy, but I can't leave you there, struggling on your own. I'll be there as soon as I can. I'm ready to fight for you. Be careful in the meantime, babe.*

When I woke up from my coma, I remembered our time together. I don't know how I came to you in that state or why my subconscious created a backstory about a residency in Charleston. I guess that I somehow knew I had to explain why I couldn't be around all the time. At any rate, I'm glad it happened and that I could support you. Your world is always surprising me. I can only imagine what other surprises lie in store for us. I'm proud to be marrying you this weekend. I love you! A single tear dropped from Brittany's eye onto the card. She looked at her grandmother and signed, "What comes next?"

Granny Mason handed her a tin plate filled with food and signed, "Saturday, come hell or high water, you need to convince Parker and Maggie to bring you to the cottage. It's best if they're with us from the beginning rather than you trying to run away and having them chase you down. Do whatever he says until you get my signal. We've got some tricks up our sleeves, designed to make them regret messing with our family. I'm going to hide now just in case they come back." She patted Brittany on the shoulder and vanished into the wind.

The breeze chilled Brittany's shoulders, which was odd for June in South Carolina, even in the morning. She took a deep breath, looking around for Parker or Maggie, thinking their energy may have been responsible for the temporary temperature drop. Thankfully, this wasn't the case. When the sun resumed its seasonally appropriate blazes, she walked down to the dock, laid back and dangled her legs in the water. Something brushed by her leg, leaving a broad ripple where it had been. Flinching, she drew her legs back onto the planks before looking down to see a school of fish. *Whew!*

Falling backward again, she watched the clouds float by one by one. Settling in for a nap, she daydreamed about Ryan. He would be here soon. Those were the best and scariest words. Brittany's short-term move to South Carolina was supposed to be a chance to spend time with her sister and niece, leading up to her new life with Ryan. She slapped the dock. *Damn it, Parker! You couldn't be satisfied with jeopardizing just one of the Nelson sisters' happiness.*

Suddenly, the dock shook, sending Brittany sailing to

the edge. Holding onto the end post, she screamed. Something pulled her leg with a strong force. She bit her lip, causing blood to gush. Tears filled her eyes as her fingers, one by one, lost their grip on the post. In an instant, something pulled her into the depths of the Intracoastal Waterway. Through the cloudy water, rocks covered in algae, seagrass and oysters created a cavern of sorts. Struggling to surge to the surface, she lost consciousness.

In her unconscious state, she had a vision of a strobing light pulling her to the shoreline. Ryan appeared, caressing her cheek and kissing her before his image faded. Susan entered the scene, hugging her and crying. "Mom? What happened to me? Where are we now?" Susan shook her head and faded just as quickly as Ryan. Then came the darkness for what seemed like days. Nothingness. *Was she dead? How would her family get rid of Parker and Maggie without her there? Did Parker kill her?*

The same strobing beam hurt her eyes again. She shielded them. Through the spaces between her fingers, she could see she was inside a house. A woman dressed in strange clothing walked over and handed her a soft robe and a pair of slippers. "You'll feel better if you put these on. My husband will wash and dry your clothes for you. We don't want you catching a cold. After all, you're gonna get rid of the Suttons for good."

Brittany gulped. "Thank you. I don't mean to be rude, but who are you; how did I get here; and how do you know about the Suttons?"

The woman looked down at her hands. "My goodness. Where are my manners? I'm Lorna. I've known Julia Caroline, uh, I mean your granny, for years. She asked us to watch out for you. We're the closest neighbors to the Suttons' cabin. Tim was out fishing earlier and saw you get pulled in by one of the um, um—" Lorna looked over her shoulders, her hands shaking.

Brittany's eyes widened. "Mermaids?"

"I wasn't sure how much your grandmother had told

you about them. The sad thing is if they knew why you were here, they'd be trying to help you instead of harm you. They're as much against the Suttons as your family, and for a good reason."

That gave Brittany an idea. She rapidly fired several questions, without pausing for a reply until the end. "Do you have the blessing? Do you know any of them? Would they listen to you?"

A tear rolled down Lorna's cheek. "Yeah, I've seen spirits ever since my mom passed when I was a child. My daughter died in the fire. She was only eight years old and visiting a friend whose mother worked at the hotel. The older women, um mermaids, have watched over her for years. They've treated her as one of their own. That's why we never leave the island. We have everything delivered to us. I couldn't bear to leave her, especially with the Sutton twins on the loose. Their spirits are among the most dangerous I've encountered. I'm so glad your family is taking care of them."

Brittany sighed. "I'm so sorry. That's horrible. I didn't realize Parker and Maggie's parents had caused so much grief in the Lowcountry. Do you think the mermaids will help us?"

Lorna wiped her tears away and stood up. "I don't just think it. I know it. Let's go talk to them."

Chapter 19

Brittany kept her stride short and calculated as they approached the dock. "I'll let you go first. I'm a little hesitant, considering what happened last time I was down here."

Lorna drew a deep breath. "Jenny, it's Mama. Come here, honey. Bring your friends with you."

The water rippled from the edge of the dock to the bank, where a girl with a long blond side ponytail adorned with a hot pink scrunchie emerged along with two women in their 20s, wearing brightly colored business suits, fanny packs and bold makeup. They didn't have a single hair out of place or water dripping from their bodies. Only their fashion sense revealed their status as fish out of the water, stuck in the 1980s for eternity.

One of the women stepped forward. "Lorna, like, why did you take our friend away? We wanted to play with her and keep her around. She seems so, like, totally awesome." *Oh, great, another group of deranged spirits, just what we need.*

Lorna walked up to her and looked her in the eye. Brittany couldn't read her lips, but whatever she said made an impression. The woman crouched, backing up a few steps.

Jenny's eyes sparkled. "Mommy! I'm so glad to see you." She wrapped her arms around her mother's waist and lay her head on her chest.

Lorna smiled. "I'm glad to see you, too. This is my

friend, Brittany. She is trying to get rid of that bad man, Parker, and his sister. She needs your help. Will you and your friends do whatever she needs?"

Jenny looked at the women, narrowing her eyes, and they nodded. "We'll get the others to help, too."

"Thank you," Brittany said. "How many friends do you have?"

The child looked off in the distance for a moment. "About 200. Yeah, that should be about right." Granny Mason's words about having safety in numbers played in her mind. The mermaids would go a long way to ensuring the Nelson sisters achieved their goal of sending Parker and Maggie away for good.

Brittany bit her lip. "Can you and your friends meet my sister at the white and gray house on Palm Court on Isle of Palms around noon on Saturday? She'll tell you everything you need to know. We're going to need all the help we can get."

The oldest mermaid rolled her eyes. "Not everyone can see us. Does your sister, like, have special powers, too?"

"Yup. She has the gift."

Jenny looked at her friends, who each nodded, and she gave Brittany a thumbs-up. "We'll be there. We can go anywhere we want for 12 hours, but after that, we wake up in the river right where we started."

Lorna clasped her hands over Brittany's. "Tim and I'll come, too. He can't see spirits, but he'll help with anything else you need. I can't believe I'm saying this, but you'd better get back inside before those devious twins get back. You've come too far to let them find out what you're planning." She waved and walked away.

A chill tingled down Brittany's back as Lorna disappeared into the wooded area in between her house and the Suttons' shack. She dreaded Parker and Maggie's return, but she needed them to come back so she could follow through with her family's plans. What if they didn't? She clenched her fists and screamed, her chest shaking. The grass crumpled under her knees as she hit the ground, bits of shell scraping and stinging her skin.

Someone placed their hand on her lower back, and Brittany spun around, prepared to take down her assailant. When she had pivoted completely, she was eye to eye with Ryan. "What are you doing here?" she signed. "Are you crazy? You shouldn't be up and moving around yet. Go to the hospital now, or go anywhere away from here. Parker will be back any minute."

"Shh." Ryan hugged her. "Paulene came to see me; she's a miracle worker. She read some words out of this ancient book and told me to drink a weird tasting smoothie. I didn't ask too many questions about what was in it, but I felt as good as new the next morning, so I hitched a ride with her. You need me to be here. I promise that I'm fine. I mean, I'm not planning to run a marathon anytime soon, but it's all good, babe."

"No. It's not." She slammed her arms against his chest. "You don't know what they're capable of. Parker murdered Nancy and almost killed Blake and Clint. Go back to the cottage. I'll never forgive myself if something happens to you. I love you way too much. Seriously. Go now!"

Ryan pulled her in close again and kissed her. Brittany's heart pounded. Being apart had affected her more than she'd realized. His strong hands massaged her neck and shoulders, melting her tension. "Everything is okay, for now, at least. Nancy and your granny found a temporary fix. Maggie and Parker are in limbo, and they will be there until midnight. They'll be pretty pissed off when they figure out what happened. You need to let me take care of you. I brought some food and other comforts from home."

Walking back into the cottage, she collapsed onto the sofa and stared at her fiancé. She should insist that he leave again. It wasn't safe for him to be here, but she didn't have the energy to argue.

Ryan sat down next to her and wrapped an arm around

her. "I've got all kinds of stuff for you. Your family is so worried. Your Mom charged your cell phone and bought a special charging case for it. It should stay charged until you get home. Blake thought you might need some toiletries. And your granny and Nancy asked me to bring you some food. Dig in, by the way."

Brittany sobbed on his shoulder. She'd missed him terribly. Is this who she and her sisters were now? If they sent Parker and Maggie away again, were they destined for them to return and wreak havoc on their lives every five years or so?

After a few moments, Ryan pulled away. "I love you. I had to see that you were okay for myself. You had me worried the last time I visited you through my, um, I guess you'd call it an out-of-body experience. But I got anxious when Blake called me and told me to come to South Carolina. I'm so glad she did, and I'm happy we're here together now, even under these weird circumstances."

She smiled weakly. "I'm glad, too. I love you, and I'm sorry you have to live through Parker's second haunting. Once was enough for me. If you're ready to run, I wouldn't blame you." She meant her words but didn't want to consider a life without Ryan.

He kissed her forehead. "You're so silly. I'm in this for life. I knew that when I met you in high school. Who knew 'worse' meant evil ghost twins would kidnap you?" He was right—this wasn't the norm for most couples.

"It's pretty ridiculous when you say it aloud. I'm glad my predicament hasn't scared you off."

Ryan shook his head. "Nope. You're stuck with me for life, babe," he signed. Locking her fingers with his, she leaned against him, drifting off to sleep.

Chapter 20

Brittany woke to Ryan's gentle touch. "Babe, we only have two hours left, and I wanted to talk to you before I have to go."

She pulled herself up so she could kiss him. "I've got something else in mind first if you think you're able."

He raised an eyebrow and took a sip of water. "Are you sure *you're* up for that? We can cuddle and talk instead."

Brittany pouted and signed, "This could be our last chance if—" What if she died? Would he marry another woman, or worse, would he live his life being sad and alone?

Ryan put out his hand. "Don't even go there. We're going to kick those Sutton twins' asses tomorrow. Your Granny and Nancy are ready for them. You and Blake are stronger than you give yourselves credit for, too." She knew he wasn't wrong, but Parker wasn't the average disgruntled ex-fiancé. Even though he was dead and had put Blake through hell on earth before he died, he'd blamed her for their relationship not working out. He was the pure definition of a narcissist, and now, he had Maggie helping him carry out his vengeance against the Nelson family.

"I never said I'm not strong. It's just that Parker killed Nancy, and she wasn't exactly weak. Now, he has a sidekick. I'm preparing you for the reality of what *could* happen."

Ryan shook his head. "I refuse to think that way, but if my beautiful fiancé wants to make love, who am I to argue

107

with her? I'll take every opportunity I can get."

"Well, in that case, hand me that toiletry bag, and I'll go freshen up." Brittany winked. She grabbed a water bottle and walked to the bathroom, where only a small shard of a mirror remained. Even in the darkness, she could see her hair had frizzed. She pulled a brush and a small tube of hair gel out of the bag. After brushing out the dozens of knots, she smoothed out the strands with a dab of hair gel. *Not great, but at least I look a little less frightening.* She splashed some water and body wash on all the critical parts of her body and dried off with her T-shirt. After brushing her teeth, she ran her tongue around them. *Ugh…Much better.* She hung her T-shirt across the shower curtain rod to dry and walked out of the bathroom.

From the kitchen, she called out, "Are you ready for me?" She walked back into the living room, and Ryan wasn't there. "Babe? Where did you go? I asked if you were ready for me. Are you hiding?" A lump formed in her throat as she became aware someone was watching her. She looked over her shoulder to see Ryan slumped over in front of the kitchen island. Parker held a knife to his neck and hissed. "Yes, we're *so* ready for you. Nice butt."

Her cheeks burned. After turning around completely, she saw Ryan's eyes were closed. He was unconscious. She screamed. "Parker! Let him go! You guys were friends when you were alive. How could you hurt him?" Even as the words left Brittany's mouth, she knew what Parker had done to Blake. Supposedly, he'd been in love with her. There was no telling what he was capable of when it came to hurting Ryan. And she wasn't about to find out.

She hurled herself toward Parker, but he stepped to the side. Her body slammed up against the corner of a sharp-edged bar height table, knocking the wind out of her. Gasping for air, she cringed as Parker dragged Ryan out of the cabin. Each time his body hit the floor, the aftershock resounded throughout Brittany's body. She clutched her stomach, tears streaming down her face, and crawled to the door, which was ajar. In the moonlight, Parker lifted him and walked toward the water. She couldn't make out where he had set him down. Brittany held onto her stomach, trying to pull herself upright, but she collapsed onto the floor again.

Granny Mason appeared, "Damn it! I don't know how, but Parker escaped. Is he back here?" Her grandmother looked her up and down. "Heaven's to Betsey, are you alright, honey? What happened? Why are you on the floor?"

Brittany shook her head and struggled to speak. "Don't worry about me! Parker's done something to Ryan. He's unconscious. They're outside. Go now!"

Granny Mason's image faded. A series of lights flashed on and off for a few seconds, finally going dark. What was that? Brittany refocused her eyes, and when the lights flickered, she saw Ryan lying across the bench seat in Clint's fishing boat. Was he still alive? Taking a deep breath, she braced herself and used the door frame to pull herself upright, stumbling to the front yard. "Parker! Don't do anything else to him! Leave him right there. He needs a doctor immediately."

Parker's evil sneer glowed in the dock light. He shrugged, snapped his fingers and leaned over to start the boat engine. The wooden boards vibrated under Brittany's feet as she ran, but the boat took off into the darkness. When she couldn't feel the engine's rumble any longer, she screamed.

Parker walked up to her and put his finger in her face. "Shut up. I don't need my annoying neighbor coming over. Anyhow, Ryan finally got what he deserved. Maggie tried to kill him in Atlanta, but you Nelson women pick the most resilient men. Well, except for me. Too bad about that. Pretty soon, you'll get yours. Now, go back inside."

Granny Mason appeared behind him, and she signed, "Sugar, Ryan will be okay. I've got this under control. Do what Parker says and no matter what, get to the house tomorrow."

With Parker's eyes locked on Brittany, she couldn't

respond to her grandmother. She turned away and walked back into the cabin, her jaw clenched. Granny would make sure Ryan got to safety, but how could she let Parker get away with what he'd done? If Brittany escaped now, it would only disrupt her family's plans. Going back into the cabin, she freshened up again and pulled on her clothing. She had given little thought to being naked in front of Parker, concerned only for Ryan's safety. But now, remembering his longing gaze repulsed her. She gagged and ran outside to throw up. Parker wasn't on the porch, but she knew he hadn't wandered off too far.

Gathering her wits, she went inside and brushed her teeth again. As she placed her toothbrush back into the bag, her hand brushed up against something smooth. *Her phone!* In the chaos, she'd forgotten about her mother sending her cell phone. She hammered out a group text to her family to see if Granny had found Ryan. Biting her lip, she waited for a response. Finally, the faithful three dots began bouncing below her message.

Blake: What are you talking about? Isn't Ryan with you?

Brittany: No! Parker knocked him out and threw him into Clint's boat. Granny is trying to catch up with him.

Blake: Don't do anything rash to Parker. Clint's going to look for Ryan, and he'll alert the Coast Guard.

Brittany fumed and paced the cabin. She couldn't sit still while Ryan drifted further out to sea, but she couldn't leave this dilapidated hovel if she wanted the madness to end. Slipping on her shoes, she ran outside and looked for Parker. He wasn't around. She refused to entertain the possibility that he was with Ryan. Instead, the grass and sand twisted beneath her feet as she made her way to the water's edge and called for Jenny.

The water swirled and rippled, and the impeccably groomed child emerged with her friends. How could she explain this to a kid? Brittany had to remind herself that Jenny wasn't an average kid—she'd been through unfathomable horrors.

Brittany smiled weakly. "Honey, I need your help. Can you please look for that nice man who came to see me earlier? He's in a boat and may be in trouble. If you find him, bring him back here or take him to my sister's house, whichever is closer."

Jenny's ponytail bobbed as she nodded. "We're on it. Let's go, girls!" They stepped back into the water and sank into the abyss as quickly as they'd come. Surely, with Clint, Granny Mason, the mermaids and the Coast Guard on the case, Ryan would come out of this frightening incident unscathed.

A gust of wind grazed Brittany's exposed neck, and she shivered. Parker appeared next to Brittany, chilling her to the core. "Why are you outside?" He smirked. "Are you worried about lover boy? I'd say he's halfway to Savannah by now, that is, if he hasn't hit another boat. That would be such a shame."

Brittany bit her tongue and cleared her throat. "You mean you weren't with him?"

Parker smoothed the wrinkles in his blazer. "No. I can't keep track of everyone who's trying to foil my plans. If the rest of your family gets up to any shenanigans, I'll send them down the river, too."

She walked away from him and toward the house, but he tapped her on the shoulder. When she turned around, he pulled her close to him. "Don't forget I'm the one in charge here, not you. Deal with it."

Brittany didn't say a word and continued walking, but she felt his eyes boring a hole into the back of her skull. When she finally made her way back into the cabin, she wept out of concern for Ryan, crying herself to sleep.

Chapter 21

Brittany's phone vibrated in her pocket, waking her. She jumped to her feet to scan the room, breathing a sigh of relief that Parker wasn't there. Squinting, she checked the message.

Blake: We're at the hospital with Ryan. Don't worry. He's just a little out of it right now because of the meds. Jenny found him before he got too far away.

Brittany clutched her chest, wiping a tear from her eye. By some miracle, Ryan was going to be okay. The proverbial brick had been lifted off her chest, and now, she might stand a chance of getting a decent night's sleep.

Brittany: Thank God! But wait, Granny wasn't with them?

Blake: I'm sure she's okay, but I'll send Nancy and Clint out to look for her.

Before slipping her phone back into her pocket, Brittany stared at the picture on her lock screen and smiled. Ryan had stuck a palm frond in her hair, dubbing her the Pineapple Princess before kissing her on the nose. They'd always promised not to take life too seriously, to trust each other and to love deeply. This moment represented many in their relationship, and Brittany believed that was the reason for their unequivocal happiness. She couldn't have handled losing Ryan. His soul was pure, and he prioritized her needs above all else. Knowing he was hurt again made her stomach hurt.

The past week had aged and tested her beyond measure. She could almost sense the crow's feet around her eyes deepening and gray hair sprouting out of her scalp. But, oddly, it was a good thing Ryan was in the hospital. She didn't need to worry about his safety during the impending battle. After everything he'd been through, his strength and resiliency were admirable, but he didn't need to be part of this mess any longer. No doubt that he'd go to the ends of the earth for her, but he shouldn't have to. She'd never asked for the ability to see and communicate with ghosts, but since it wasn't a choice, she was glad she had the power to send them on to their next destination. And she wouldn't rest until she knew flames had engulfed all twenty of Parker and Maggie's toes for eternity. *Just one more day.* The welcome thought brought on a sense of peacefulness, and before too long, she drifted off to sleep.

A burst of cool air sent Brittany's hand, searching for the edges of the worn quilt. Shivering, she covered herself, checked her phone and saw a missed text.

Blake: Granny isn't back. Clint, Elaina and Nancy have been trying to find her all night. Do you think your mermaid friends would look for her?

Brittany ran to the dock and called for Jenny, but no one appeared. She turned around and ran along the shoreline, pleading for help, but no one came. A flickering light in the distance beckoned her. Maybe it was coming from Lorna and Tim's house. They might know how to get Jenny's attention. With her grandmother's spirit at risk, she had to ask. Mosquitoes swarmed, nipping at her shoulders as the quilt slid to the ground. She swatted the pests, not allowing them to slow her stride. Roots pulled at her feet, but her adept footwork navigated the dark forest floor.

Sure enough, the light on their front porch glowed a brilliant gold, flashing on and off with no apparent pattern. Was the flickering because of faulty wiring, or was someone trying to send a message? Brittany pounded on the door.

Lorna opened it, dripping with sweat and her hand on her chest. "Jenny's missing. We walked down to the water to kiss her goodnight, and she didn't come. None of her friends came for us, either. I'm so worried. She's never done this. We've been flicking the porch light switch to get your grandmother's attention. Usually, she comes right away. Suppose something bad has happened to Jenny. Well, I—just don't know what on earth I'll do." Lorna wiped a tear from her cheek.

"Granny is missing, too. Where could they be?" Brittany scratched her head.

"I think I know, but you won't like it. Come with me." Lorna picked up a flashlight and a hunting knife. Brittany's eyes widened, and her new friend shook her head. "There are snakes and all kinds of other critters out there. I'd rather be safe than sorry."

The two women made their way down a winding path behind the house. Lorna held back branches for Brittany. Decaying leaves crumbled beneath Brittany's feet, and nerves and hunger pangs stabbed her stomach. After a few minutes, they came to a small pond. Brittany scanned the landscape as much as possible in the pitch-black environment. "Are they here?" Brittany asked, unable to see. "Use your flashlight. I can't read your lips in the dark." Something pulled at Brittany's ankles, bringing her down to the ground. *What just happened?* Winded, she tried to pull herself up, but someone knocked her onto her back. "Lorna? Is that you? You're hurting me!"

A bright light blinded Brittany momentarily, but as her eyes focused, she saw that Lorna was kneeling on top of her, focusing the flashlight's beam on her mouth.

"What are you doing?" Brittany shifted her weight back and forth, attempting to free herself, but Lorna shook her head furiously. Had Lorna lost her mind?

"I feel terrible about doing this to you, but the mermaids have decided they want to keep you. They've hidden Jenny from me, and the only way they'll free her is if I give you to them. Again, I'm so sorry. You seem to be a nice girl. I promise to watch after you after they claim you. I'll let your Granny know where you are so she can stay in touch with you." She pressed the knife to Brittany's neck; pressure from the blade threatened to slice through her sweat-covered skin.

Brittany pulled the knife out of Lorna's hand and rolled out from underneath her. Gathering her bearings, she ran through the darkness. *It would help if I could hear this psycho's footsteps!* The cold air filled her contracting lungs, but she knew she couldn't stop, not yet. *I never thought I'd be looking forward to going back to that damn shack.* She worked her way through the lush greenery, and finally, the rundown cabin appeared before her. Every bone in her feet ached, and she longed for a hot bath and one of Ryan's famous foot massages. But she had to keep going until she'd made her way through this pocket of forest.

Brittany stopped in the clearing long enough to catch her breath and loosen a cramp in her ankle. Looking over her shoulder, she didn't see anyone, so Brittany sprinted for the shack. It wasn't much of a hiding place, but at least the doors and windows locked. As she turned her head, she was face to face with Parker and Maggie. *Crap!*

He grabbed Brittany's ponytail, pulling her to the cabin. She screamed for help, but no one came. Not even Lorna. *Where did that bitch go?* That was a harsh thought about someone trying to protect her daughter, even if the child was dead and lived at the bottom of a river. Wouldn't Blake do the same to safeguard Macy? *Wouldn't I?*

Brittany tried to free herself from Parker's grasp, but she couldn't. He pulled her into the shack, slamming and locking the door behind them. *Oh, God, what comes next?*

Pushing her onto the couch, Maggie yelled at her. "Just what did you think you were doing? Were you trying to escape? Aww...how adorable! Did you think that wishy-washy woman had enough gumption to take you away from here? She knows better than to pull that shit. I'd erase that wisp of a child of hers in a heartbeat. Those pathetic mermaids have no power individually. They depend on each other to source as much magic as I have in my baby finger. Combine my power with Parker's; there's no comparison!"

Parker glowered at her, eating up his sister's words as if he were tasting the most delicious meal of his life. "Of course, they'd love to have you or one of your sisters, not that we'd give you to them. At least, we won't yet. If you run out your usefulness, we might turn you over to them. Just so you know, you're no good to them unless you're dead, so don't push your luck with me. Sit on the sofa until we tell you to move again. Got it?" Parker crossed his arms, pivoted, and walked through the door. Maggie chuckled as she followed him outside.

Brittany wanted to hit them or to make them feel pain, but there wasn't much she could do at the moment. Ghosts didn't experience pain the same way as humans. Instead, she cleared her mind as much as possible and attempted to meditate. In mere hours, her family would put an end to this nonsense, hopefully, for good.

Chapter 22

⤳

The night had come and gone, but Brittany had failed to drift off to sleep. She gave up on resting when the sunrise sent its fiery glow through the shack, painting every dust-covered surface a brilliant orange. She pulled herself off the couch and looked outside. The choppy water reflected the sky's ember tones. Suddenly, a tire-sized ripple drew her attention. *Was that a mermaid preparing to surface?* A cold chill tingled down her spine, and she shivered.

There was no sign of Lorna or the Sutton twins. Where had they gone? Maggie and Parker had to come back; otherwise, her family's plans would be foiled. She refused to entertain that idea. It was their turn to suffer. With family on her mind, she grabbed her phone to text Blake to find out if their grandmother had turned up yet.

Blake: Nope. We're getting anxious now. Nancy can't reach her through the spiritual network.

Brittany's heart palpitated. This was the first time Nancy hadn't been able to find Granny. Their network worked almost like GPS, allowing them to sense each other's location. They'd always had a special connection because they were so close in life, almost sisters. The best friends had vowed to watch over each other's families should one of them die before the other.

Brittany: When Parker and Maggie come back, I'll try to

dig up the truth. In the meantime, I'll dive into this room full of books again. Hopefully, there's an answer in there.

Blake: Be careful not to push their buttons too hard. We need them to bring you here today. I can feel it in my bones that Granny's okay.

Please, God, let her be right! They all needed Granny. Even in her spectral form, she exuded positivity and love. Having a matriarch bigger than life itself had shaped the Nelson women's lives in many inexplicable ways. They were stronger, more resilient and kinder for it. The sisters had been through hell and back together, fighting for their family's lives. They had lost Nancy's earthly form, but she'd found her way back to them. Brittany was thankful for that. Macy needed her great-grandma, and Blake needed her navigator.

Pushing her way into Maggie's morose den of books, she searched through the mountainous stacks, thumbing through worn covers and pages. Most of the books covered how to resurrect banished spirits and bring them back from the Other Side. A dog-eared page caught her attention. The hairs on her arm stood up on end as she read the chapter title—*Hiding a Spirit in Plain Sight: The Bottling Spell.*

No effing way! Parker and Maggie had hidden her Granny! Brittany's blood boiled, sending an inferno pulsating through her veins. She exhaled and focused her attention on the text:

You can send spirits to a holding place in case you need their powers in the future. To "bottle" their essence, simply lead them to a place they love or near a person they care about. Find an object in which you can trap them and say, "Leave the earth for a short while, gravitate in this object. This is not your final destination." With this particular incantation, they will only remain inside the object for a month at a time before being automatically released.

Should you want to release them beforehand, simply take the object and sprinkle the tears or blood of their loved ones over the top of the item while repeating the phrase, 'You are

*free from your cell—return to earth, not Heaven or Hell,'
three times. You can send them back to the depths of the item
of your choice for another month.*

The book fell off Brittany's lap, and she ran into the
living room, searching for anything that might contain her
devoted grandmother's spirit. Nothing in the aging, decrepit
shack seemed worthy of holding Granny Mason as a
prisoner. Maybe that was the point. Parker wouldn't respect
their beloved grandmother to keep her in a beautiful perfume
atomizer or an Austrian crystal vase. No—it was just as
likely she was being held captive inside a cigar box or a
cheap wine bottle. Despite the chapter name, she doubted that
the Sinister Suttons would leave the item out in the open,
making it easy for retrieval. They were too smart for their
own good.

A stray mosquito flew through the window and bit
Brittany's neck as she paced. She swatted the pest; something
was missing—her necklace! Running to the sofa, she dug in
the nooks and crannies around the cushions. Then, she
examined every inch of the kitchen, bathroom and book-
filled back room. She hadn't taken the necklace off on
purpose. Her stomach churned, and acid bubbled up into her
throat. Could Parker have taken it? Had he imprisoned her
grandmother inside its chain or pendant? Where would he
hide it? Definitely not in the shack. He would have known
that she'd find it. And the cottage wasn't likely either. If
Blake had found it there, she would have known something
was amiss. Why did he have to be so clever?

Realizing she hadn't drunk water or eaten that day, she
took a moment to clear her mind and consume some of
Blake's homemade cornbread with peanut butter. It was an
odd combination, but they didn't need refrigerated in the
short term, and the peanut butter energized her. A full
stomach brightened her disposition ever so slightly. Calmed
and refreshed, she closed her eyes, intending to rest for only a
moment. However, the restless night had taken its toll on
Brittany, and she allowed her body to close out the rest of the

world and dream about a Parker-free existence. The sun sparkled more; the skies were a more brilliant blue, and best of all, her family smiled more. A peacefulness came over her, and she laughed more genuinely than she had in almost a decade. Today was a day of reckoning for the Suttons. Her family was finally free.

But like dreams often do, the tone changed, growing colder and darker. Brittany's dreams shifted to a familiar place, a cavern of sorts. Misshapen rock structures sprouted from the ground, and a filmy blue substance filled the air. A vibrant yellow creature zoomed past her shoulder, disappearing into a dark corner. What was that? A bird? An alien? Scanning the room, she attempted to draw a breath, but she choked on bubbles. What kind of dream is this?

The brightly colored creature came back into the light. Brittany squinted, but then her eyes widened—it was a fish! She was underwater in the mermaids' lair! Clearly, this guy wanted her to follow him. Obliging, she navigated the passage's tight nooks and crannies, scraping her hands on the coral. Blood trickled from her fingers, leaving red trails behind her. The fish stopped in front of a natural shelf, filled with intricate shells, including oysters, embedded on the massive rock. Her new friend emphasized a specific section of the shelf, worn smooth with iridescent grayish purple bands. One oyster, in particular, stood out from the rest. Its texture and sheen were more pronounced. Was Granny Mason trapped inside? Brittany picked up the shell with trembling hands and began examining it.

Darkness filled the makeshift room, and the fish slowly backed away, slipping into the crevice between two boulders. Its squinted eyes glowed. Brittany wished she could join him, but she'd have to face whatever was coming her way. After rolling up her sleeves, she tucked the shell into her pocket and waited for the evil presence to reveal itself.

Parker's sneer appeared first, then the rest of his face, and eventually, his body. "What's in your pocket? Family doesn't keep secrets from each other. Hand it over to me."

Ugh! Why does Parker have to haunt my dreams?
Brittany pushed him. "No! You're not my family! Go to hell!"

"No, thanks," Parker licked his lips and flashed a smile. "Hell's not very nice this time of year. I much prefer Maine. The weather's more hospitable in Bar Harbor on these blazing hot days. Now, hand it over, Brittany. I know you have something."

"I wouldn't do that in a million years. Screw you!" Brittany took off running aimlessly, looking ahead to make sure she wouldn't accidentally slip on a flounder and head-butt a shark. That wouldn't help her day, or this dream, get any better. Not seeing Parker, she hid in a secluded area to examine the mollusk.

"Hey, Granny, are you in there?"

Nothing happened, but she wasn't sure what to expect. She examined the beautiful shell, waiting for something…anything to happen. "Granny, give me some kind of sign to let me know it's you." *Get a grip, girl. Your grandmother isn't inside an oyster. Granny's inside your necklace, remember?* She shook her head, laughing at herself, but when she set the shell down on a rock, its gray and aubergine exterior transformed into an iridescent lavender. Her heart in her throat, she picked it up again and placed it in her pocket. If her lovely grandmother was inside, how would they free her?

Hopefully, Maggie's books would spell out the details, and the curse wouldn't prove difficult to undo. The Nelson sisters could see and communicate with spirits, but they weren't witches. Their only attempt at magic, if you could call it that, was the blessing ceremony where they'd sent Parker on to his so-called final resting place. Now, they needed to pull off more than they'd ever bargained for, but the safety of their family made the quest worthwhile.

A shadow darkened the nook, and Brittany looked up to see Parker reaching out for her. She ducked and swam away, not stopping until she came to a dead end. Parker's eyes pierced holes into the back of her head. She turned, and face-to-face with the monster, and he lunged for her.

Brittany woke covered in sweat, her heart racing. *What a dream!* Standing up to stretch, something heavy jiggled in her pocket. She didn't have to put her hand inside to know it was the oyster. But how did something transport through a dream to reality? *What a weird twist of events, even by her family's standards!* She walked back to Maggie's room and flipped through the book to confirm the directions, which called for tears or blood of the prisoner's loved ones. Brittany had never been one for crying, but her heart had been heavy over the past week. Hopefully, she'd be able to conjure up some tears on the spot; she wasn't in the mood for stabbing herself. Closing her eyes, she focused on recent events. Over the past seven days, the Sinister Suttons had kidnapped and terrorized at least half of her family members in some form or fashion. Wasn't that enough to bring on the waterworks?

Her stomach churned, and a familiar tightness formed in her eyes and throat. The inevitable tears spilled down her cheeks and onto the sleek, silvery, lilac ridges. Brittany kissed the shell and fist-pumped with it in her palm. *Okay, Granny. Let's do this.* She started, *"You are free from your cell. Return to earth, not Heaven or Hell."* She repeated the phrase, stopping to look at its exterior. *Ugh, nothing has happened yet.* She started the third round, and just as the word, *earth,* escaped her lips, a frigid breeze swept over the room. Pages of the books flapped, and Parker's devilish face appeared. "I don't know what's inside this thing, but I know you want it, so it must be powerful." He grabbed the oyster shell out of her hands, pushed her down onto the floor, hovering an inch from her face before he vanished.

Chapter 23

B rittany ran to her phone to call Blake via video chat. The phone shook in her hands while she waited for her sister to answer. *Blake! Answer the damn phone!* Brittany's pulse quickened, and her stomach knotted. How were they going to fight the Suttons without Granny Mason? She was the family's fearless leader and had the most experience dealing with extreme hauntings. They stood little chance of putting an end to the terror without her by their side.

Her phone lit up with an incoming video call from Blake. As soon as Brittany saw her sister's face, she frantically signed, "Parker has Granny." Brittany filled Blake in on her dream and the events that had followed.

"We can't fight Maggie and him without her. They'll kill all of us." A tear rolled down Blake's flushed face. Wiping it away, she signed, "Sorry."

Brittany's mouth gaped. "Don't go there. We've just gotta think creatively. There's gotta be a way."

Blake rubbed her temples. "Well, there is one thing that worked on Parker last time, but you're going to hate me for suggesting it." That didn't sound great. What could her sister possibly recommend?

"Geez, what?" Brittany groaned. "I'll do anything I have to at this point." *Hopefully, I won't have to do anything too crazy!*

"Yeah, well, remember how he cooperated with me when I flirted with him? You know, he's convinced that you had a massive crush on him. I bet you could make him think you're in love with him."

"Ack! That's disgusting. Do I have to?" Brittany gagged and coughed but then pulled herself together. "Alright, I'll figure something out."

"From what Nancy says, you don't have to worry about anything *too* gross happening. He doesn't have use of *all* of his bodily functions unless there is a full moon. Luckily, that ship has sailed. Whatever you do, don't forget to get him here by 1 o'clock at the latest."

Brittany put a hand on her hip. "As Granny says, we'll be there, come hell or high water."

Ending the video call, she sighed. She hoped her act of seduction would work on Parker. Having been with Ryan since high school, she hadn't needed to worry about attracting other men, let alone ghosts. What if she didn't have a knack for it? *At any rate, this is going to be a long morning.*

Brittany scavenged the kitchen for the last edible remnants of her family's provisions. No amount of planning would help her prepare for Parker's return, but she had to work on her acting skills. Stroking his ego would prove to be no easy feat. Rehearsing what she was going to say, she was grateful she didn't have to hear the despicable lies coming out of her mouth. She pushed down the bile that threatened to vacate her esophagus and drew a deep breath.

As much as she wanted to avoid seeing Lorna or the mermaids, she needed to get some fresh air, even for just a few minutes. Opening the door, she took in a deep breath and let the sunshine beam down on her face. A crane swooped down to snag fish out of the sparkling blue water. How could such a beautiful place house evil creatures? Her heart ached, picturing Jenny being held captive by the older mermaids. The child didn't deserve mistreatment from those witches. Brittany understood why Lorna would kill her to save her daughter's spirit, especially when she hadn't saved the girl's life during the hotel fire. No parent should have to live with that guilt day in, day out.

Against Brittany's better judgment, she walked up to the edge of the water and called for her friend. The river was smooth, not a ripple in sight. What could she say to get the other mermaids' attention? *Ugh.* "Hey, y'all, come and get me if you want me that bad. Just let the kid go."

Bubbles fizzed up through the glassy surface, and a mermaid popped up, fully decked out in her 80s garb, not a shoulder pad out of place. "Okay, so, like, you've got my attention. I'm listening." She chewed her bubble gum and adjusted her wire-rimmed glasses.

"What have you done to Jenny? Don't feed me any B.S., just the truth." These mermaids were intimidating, but Brittany didn't want them to sense her fear. Instead, she crossed her arms and narrowed her eyes.

Smirking, the mermaid blew a watermelon-scented bubble. "She'll be fine. She just needs to stop running her mouth, tryin' to tell us what to do. Why would we ever put a kid in charge? So, what's this about us coming to get you? Did you give up on being alive? Did a boy break your heart or somethin'?"

"No—Lorna said you wouldn't free Jenny until you had me. She tried to kill me last night so she could make the trade."

The mermaid threw her head back, laughing. "We're not that particular that it has to be you. It's just that we want some more power. If you've got someone else in mind to take your spot, you can try to convince us."

Brittany bit her lip. "I think we can work something out at my sister's house. Are y'all still planning to come today?" Having the mermaids around would be a double-edged sword. The Nelson sisters would have to watch them at all times to make sure they didn't try anything shady.

"If you're promising to help us strengthen our underwater army, we'll be there. But one thing, don't go back on your part of the deal, or you and the girl will have to pay. Got it?"

Brittany gulped and nodded. "We'll make it happen." She walked back into the house to check her phone—no missed texts. To make the most of the situation, she went to Maggie's room and took photos of the contents of books that might prove helpful during what promised to be a horrific evening at the Mason B&B. So much for coming to South Carolina to help her sister run their family's business and help care for Macy. Life had become exponentially worse for Blake since Brittany had arrived. Sure, Maggie could have found another way to bring Parker back, but it would have been more difficult without Brittany's carelessness. Shielding her eyes, Brittany checked her phone—only two-and-a-half hours to go. *Was her grandmother okay? Damn it, Suttons!* She punched her palm. *They'd better get their sorry asses back to this shack in time to leave.* She clutched her rumbling stomach and took a few healing breaths. There was nothing to do but wait for them to show up.

The front porch, bathed in a warm glow, invited her to sit and unwind. Tapping her foot to a familiar rhythm, she tried to unravel its origins. She might not be able to hear music, but she could often feel the rhythm of songs. This was different somehow. Years of singing with her grandmother had embedded the beats in her mind, her heart. Closing her eyes, she allowed her memories to take her back to every moment music had played a significant role in her life. With each breath she took, another line of lyrics played in her mind. Then, it came to her; Granny Mason had sung the song throughout her childhood, tapping her foot and signing the words as she belted them. After each impromptu performance, her grandmother would spin Brittany around the room, and they would curtsy before falling over on the sofa, laughing. The last time Granny Mason sang to Brittany, she signed, "I love you. Never forget that or the words to this song. Promise me."

Brittany had laughed, but after seeing her grandmother frown, she nodded. "I'll always remember you and our song." She hadn't thought about the song in years. It hadn't been forgotten but stored away for this very moment. Maybe it was more than just a memory. She considered the meaning woven into the chorus—*Dance into the wind, my friend. Fly and shine. Wherever you go, know you are mine.*

Why was this important to Julia Caroline? Brittany rubbed her temples. Where was Granny when you needed her help? *Oh yeah, Parker trapped her inside an effing oyster shell.*

Chapter 24

Someone tapped Brittany on the shoulder, bringing her back to reality. *Ugh, Parker!* Couldn't he have just stayed away until time to leave for the cottage?

He flicked a cigarette butt in her direction, and she jumped. "What the actual—?" she started.

"You can't talk to me like that, bitch," Parker said through his teeth. "I'm the boss here; don't forget it." He strutted off toward the water and crossed his arms, looking off in the distance.

It was time to put her acting skills to the test. Brittany numbed herself, holding down the vomit brewing in her stomach as she walked up to Parker. Placing her hand on her hip, she batted her eyes at him. "Hey, my bad. I'm sorry. I was asleep, and you scared me. That's all. I've been thinking about us some more, and I wanted to run a few ideas past you."

Parker's eyes widened in suspicion. "Yeah, right? What about Ryan?"

She nodded. "Well, you took care of him. Remember? He's gone. I was only marrying him for financial security, anyway." Brittany grabbed ahold of his shirt collar, kissing him. His icy lips chilled her to the core, but she couldn't stop now. "Why don't we talk about what we want out of this relationship? What are you looking for?"

His green eyes danced. "I need a companion who doesn't mind taking Blake down. I have a hard time believing you will hurt your sister but don't worry. I want the satisfaction of tormenting her myself. All I need you to do is make sure she doesn't leave and her pathetic husband doesn't try to save the day. Do you think you can handle that?"

She cleared her mind and smiled. "I'll do anything for you. I had such a huge crush on you when Blake first started dating you. The night you tried to make your move on me, I was afraid she would find out. She was so jealous of me back then. I had to pretend like I didn't want to be with you."

"If what you're saying is true, I shouldn't have ever been with her. It was you all along. I might still be alive if I'd chosen the right sister. No matter. I've enjoyed this new life. I can travel wherever and whenever I want, and I don't have to worry about sleeping or eating. Just so you know, I can still do a lot of the *activities* I used to, and several ladies have told me I'm surprisingly good at them. Of course, the women have to see me to appreciate all I have to offer, but there's a shocking number of empaths in the Lowcountry who don't mind a little paranormal action. I'm a little more limited in the frequency, but I make up for it. Quality over quantity. You might be surprised by what I can still do." He winked at her.

Brittany swallowed the fire bubbling in her throat. She couldn't throw up right now, regardless of Parker's disgusting proposition. Forcing a smile, she lay her head on his shoulder. "I can't wait to find out. Have you seen my grandma around lately? I need to make sure I can't get pregnant...this will be my first experience with a spirit, and I don't have my birth control with me."

He shook his head. "I haven't seen her since she was nosing around here a couple of days ago." What a freaking creep. No question: he'd kidnapped and hidden her grandmother. His blatant lies didn't surprise Brittany, but she'd hoped her romantic advances would lead to him cracking, even if just a little.

Parker grabbed her hand and kissed it. Brittany resisted the urge to gag and tried to listen. "Don't worry about your

129

contraceptives. Even if I could get you pregnant, I can't have sex right now. Sadly, we must wait. I promise to make it worth your while." Brittany shivered. *Thank God Blake and Nancy were right!*

Forcing a smile, Brittany creaked out the unimaginable. "Hey, do you want to cuddle for a while?" He followed her into the shack, and they plopped down on the couch together. As he wrapped his arm around her, the worn sofa springs pinched her butt cheeks. He brushed her face with a hand, and goosebumps lined her arms. This was her nightmare but a necessary evil.

Afraid of what would happen next, she prepared to distract him from his romantic advances for a few moments. She leaned back so she could see Parker's face. "Are you ready to go take Blake down today?"

Parker's eyes widened. "Why are you in such a hurry?"

"I want to get it over with, so we can focus on us. Until my family is a distant memory, I don't think I'll be able to perform in the bedroom. I mean, you and Blake were engaged. And with everything you two have been through, I just need to put it all past us." Brittany placed her hand on his upper thigh.

"Say no more. We'll get rid of your sister before dinner today." Parker stood up. "But first, I need to let Maggie know so she can be there, too. I'll be back soon, lover." He vanished into nothingness, and Brittany sighed with relief— her drama electives in college must have paid off!

When the Sutton twins returned to the shack, Maggie appeared inches from Brittany's face. Her mouth moved, but she was too close for Brittany to read her thin, scaly lips.

Brittany waved. "Can you move back like four feet? Remember, I can't hear you." She looked around to see if Parker was watching, but he must have stayed outside.

Maggie rolled her smoldering green eyes but moved across the room. "If you are lying to Parker about helping us, I'll break every bone in your body and crush each of them into a fine powder. You won't die immediately, but you'll welcome death when it arrives. I'm tired of your family's crap already, and I'm not letting you Nelson bitches do anything else to jeopardize Parker and me being back together again."

Brittany stared at her. "You're just jealous that Parker will be happy again. He'll be getting it on the regular, and you'll be over in your sad little corner feeling sorry for yourself. Go screw yourself." Maggie glared at Brittany, who smirked and continued. "It's your turn to read my lips. You were right about one thing. I am a bitch. Here are a few other things you should know. Men can't resist me. I always get what I want. I'll have your brother eating out of the palm of my hand in no time. And I can destroy you in so many other ways. As my granny always says, there's more than one way to skin a cat. In case it isn't clear, you'd be the cat. Don't forget it."

Watching Maggie skulk off into her room and slam the door behind her, Brittany laughed. Maybe enjoying this moment was cold-hearted, but after everything the Suttons had put her family through, they deserved whatever brutal punishment they had coming to them. Brittany believed in karma; it was just a matter of time.

Parker walked into the living room with an arched eyebrow. "Did I hear yelling?"

"Your sister threatened me, so I reminded her I'm pretty badass myself. She learned a little lesson, and I think we're all the better for it. It's good it happened now."

Parker shook his head. "That's not the right attitude for either of you to have. You guys need to try to get along. After all, pretty soon, she'll be the only family you have, other than me."

What a horrible thought! Brittany choked back tears and pulled the corners of her mouth into a slight smile. "That's right; we'll be sisters." The bizarre concept was almost too much to bear, but they were closing in on time to go to the cottage where her family would fix everything amiss.

Parker walked back into the dark hallway to collect Maggie, and they joined Brittany on the couch. Sitting down, he stared at Brittany. "You both need to promise me we're going to work together, not against each other today. You know there is strength in numbers in all supernatural matters. Can you both act like adults?" Maggie glared at Brittany like a predator ready to pounce on its prey, but she revealed her pearly white teeth and nodded. "Anything for you, Bub." *Bub? As in Bubba? Yuck! Why did they have pet names for each other?* Parker tilted his head toward Brittany. "Are you game? Can you get along?"

Brittany nodded. "Totally. I'll do whatever it takes." Standing behind Parker, Maggie scowled and pretended to put her finger down her throat and heave. She finished her performance by flipping off Brittany with both hands. But it didn't matter—not one bit. After all, Brittany and her family were going to take the Suttons down, making sure they suffered beyond measure for every moment of torment, heartache, concern and inconvenience they'd ever caused their family.

Oblivious to Maggie's immature antics, Parker pursed his lips. "Good." He pulled out a bronze pocket watch and examined it as if he were studying fine art. "We're going to leave at precisely 11:30." He looked at Brittany. "That gives you about an hour to rest up. You'd better try to squeeze in a nap. We don't know how late this fight will go. We need you feeling sharp and ready to take down the entire world if need be."

Brittany shot him a smile. *Yes, this will be quite the fight. You have no idea.*

Chapter 25

Darkness enveloped the shack; the eclipse was underway. Brittany tapped her feet in time to her grandmother's song on the front porch until someone placed their hand on her shoulder. *Was it Parker or Maggie? Did it matter?* Resisting the urge to elbow them in the groin, she took their hand instead. It was Parker. In one smooth motion, they took flight. Her teeth chattered as they ascended, but there was no warming herself.

The beacon of the Sullivan's Island Lighthouse glowed in the distance. The juxtaposition of a dark sky before noon was hard to process, but here they were, soaring through the pitch black. Realizing she was holding her breath, Brittany exhaled. Everything had to go okay; her family had been through enough.

Descending, she braced herself for the odd sensations and supernatural battle to come. As her feet hit the ground, her eyes adjusted to the scenery that lay ahead. The Mason homestead, now Blake and Clint's home, had seen more than its fair share of pain and conflict, but it still stood firm, protective of its family, just like any obstinate Southern woman.

Parker grabbed her hand and pulled her to a streetlight. "Go get your sister and her *perfect* husband, so we can get this party started." He slapped Brittany on the butt. She bit her tongue and walked away. Tasting blood, Brittany fumed, but she couldn't retaliate, not yet.

Brittany walked to the second-floor den to collect her family. They jumped up from their seats, but she frantically

133

signed, warning them not to use their voices. "Hey, Parker is waiting for you guys. This is going to sound crazy, but he has trapped Granny inside an oyster shell. And he thinks I'm going to help him kill you. Follow my lead and trust me. I've got a plan. Abandon the cleansing ceremony unless this new plan goes awry. Trust me. I'm 99.9% sure this will work out better."

Everyone nodded, but the concern in their eyes tugged at Brittany's heart. *Suck it up. There's no time to be emotional.* Shaking off her nerves, she sprang into action and motioned for her family to join her. Turning to Blake, she asked about Macy and Ryan. Neither of them had any business being at the cottage during the inevitable war between good and evil.

"I sent Macy to Clint's brother's house in Columbia. And by some miracle, Ryan is doing okay at the hospital. I didn't want either of them to be here, just in case…" Blake trailed off.

Brittany hugged her sister. Pulling away from her, she signed. "Thank God! That's the best news I've had all day."

Nancy stood in the corner, wringing her hands. "Hon, do you know which one of them has Julia Caroline?"

Brittany shook her head. "Parker took the oyster shell from me, but he's acting like he hasn't seen Granny in days. But he's such an effing liar, who knows? I've got a plan to get Granny back. The cleansing ceremony didn't fix our problems last time, and I don't think it will now. Just follow my lead, no matter what I do. Trust me. Now, let's go give the Sinister Suttons what they deserve."

One by one, the Nelsons and Parsons followed Brittany to the garden. Cloaked in darkness, the evil twins' eyes glowed similar to those of cats on the prowl. Brittany gulped—*this was it*. The devious duo had busted Parker out of his so-called final resting place last time. Brittany and her family needed a more foolproof solution this time around.

Taking a deep breath, she walked up to Parker and put her arms around his neck. "Hey, there. I missed you." She kissed his cheek and turned to her family. "I have an announcement. Parker and I are together now. I've spent too many years denying my attraction to him, and I'm finally ready to be happy. I know you guys probably don't understand this, but luckily, you won't have to live with it for too long."

Parker chuckled. "Blake, how does it feel to see me with another woman? I hope it's eating you up inside. We could have had all of this, but you snooze, you lose." He grabbed Brittany by the waist, and she leaned into him.

Blake walked closer to them. "Parker, you're the one who got away, but if you make my sister happy, that's awesome." Clint balled his fists but otherwise stood still.

Something glowed from inside Parker's pocket. *Could it be the oyster shell?* How could she retrieve it without him noticing? Trying not to gag, she pressed her body firmly into his, massaging his waist and upper thighs, letting her hands explore his body until she reached his pockets. She slid her hand under the shell, rubbing his leg. When she was sure she had his full attention, she kissed him passionately. *What was I thinking? Please, God, let Ryan forgive me.* The contents of her stomach swirled around at a maddening speed, threatening to spew everywhere. But she had Parker where she wanted him. Continuing to kiss him, she carefully slid the shell out of his pocket and placed it inside her own.

Maggie stepped forward. "What was that all about? I thought I heard something out front, so I checked, but no one was there." Glaring at Brittany, she grimaced. "Why do you want to be with her?"

Parker pulled away from Brittany and stared at his sister. "What's it to you? You've never taken an interest in my personal life before. Why should you now? We're dead. In case you haven't noticed, there aren't a lot of dating options for us. It's not like I can exactly download an online dating app. Plus, Brittany is smoking hot and smart. Trust me. She is going to help us."

Maggie rolled her eyes. "Wow. Do you think she has

your best interests at heart? This family isn't worried about anything but their own selfish needs. Just you wait. She'll turn on you in a heartbeat."

"That's not true. Take it back and apologize to Brittany."

"Not on your life, and especially not on hers," Maggie spat in Brittany's direction. "Screw you and your entire pathetic family. Parker, you're truly a disgrace to the Sutton name."

While the twins bickered inches away from each other, Brittany signed to Blake. "I have the oyster. I'm just waiting for the right moment to free Granny Mason."

Blake bit her lip. "Britt, be so careful. To be honest, I'm kinda freaking out about all of this." She wiped a tear from her cheek.

"Get a grip. There's no time to worry! We'd better act like we care what's going on between the demented duo over there." Brittany pointed toward Parker and Maggie, who were shoving each other like a couple of six-year-olds.

"Whoa." Blake mouthed. "I thought they were adults when they both died."

Brittany stifled a laugh and covered her mouth. They were pretty ridiculous, but their immature fight was buying them some time for the next part of her plan.

Clint, who had been waiting in the wings, joined them, putting an arm on each of their shoulders. "So, what's next? Are we going to watch Dumb and Dumber smack each other around all night? If so, I'm going to need to grab a beer."

"Hush…we're biding our time. Where did everyone else go?" Brittany asked.

"Gram heard something, so Elaina and your mom went to investigate the front yard with her." Clint wiped the sweat from his brow. "How is it so hot without the sun shining?"

"Of course, it's hot." Blake fanned herself. "In South Carolina, it's as hot as hades year-round, even in January."

"Hey, you guys, I think we've got bigger fish to fry." Clint gestured behind Blake and Brittany.

As Brittany turned, her jaw dropped. Nearly 200 people gathered in the garden, appearing almost simultaneously out of thin air. *The mermaids!* Jenny ran to Brittany to hug her. "We're here to help you, but then, you have to give Serena, our leader, what she wants."

Parker and Maggie were still arguing, oblivious to their guests, until a lightning bolt struck the ground beside them, singeing the nearby greenery. Parker's eyes narrowed, and his face reddened. He stared at Brittany. "Who are all these people, and what are they doing here?"

"Sweetie, they're just here to help us find our grandmother. You know the lady who you said you hadn't seen in days? So, you really don't know where she is?" Brittany twirled her ponytail.

Parker shook his head. "Seriously. I have no idea. That old bat has been all over the place ever since I died. She probably was before then, but I wasn't open to seeing the supernatural while I was alive. I was too busy working and living my life."

Brittany smiled. "Isn't that a nice sentiment—living your life? That's something you've never been content to allow any of us Nelson women to do. We'd like to have normal lives where we go shopping and on vacations with our significant others without worrying if some narcissistic bully of a stalker will show up and ruin our day. If you had any decency, you'd disappear, but I guess that mama of yours didn't have time to teach you any manners while she worked all day. Wait a minute. She didn't work; she is your daddy's little trophy wife, so what's her excuse for raising two horrible children like you and Maggie?"

"Amen to all of that, but you forgot to call him a cheat and a liar. He cheated on me with Sharon, and now he's lying to us about Granny Mason," Blake said.

Parker threw his hands up in the air. "Stop talking about my parents like that. You don't understand what they went through after the hotel burned down," he barked at Brittany. Turning to Blake, he spat, "I can't do anything about having cheated on you while I was alive. But I don't have an effing clue why you two keep going on about the old biddy."

Brittany pulled the shell out of her pocket. "You mean to tell me you weren't the one who trapped her inside this? Lie your ass off, but I saw the books in Maggie's room at the shack. The bottling spell probably did the trick, and pretty easily from the sounds of it."

"Honestly, I didn't touch your grandmother. Maggie was right. You only care about your family, you selfish bitch! You know I've never had a problem fessing up to anything I've done. Just like right now, I'm going to set the damn cottage on fire. Say goodbye to all of your family's precious memories." Parker stretched out his arms, and red beams of light shot out from his fingertips, just how Blake had described the horrific scene of Nancy's death. Flames cascaded up and down the trellis on the screened-in porch, inching their way up the fascia.

Chapter 26

Brittany's heart pounded. Fearless to a fault, burning to death had been her only phobia. As a child, she'd experienced a close call with a fire at her daycare. Ever since then, the thought of dying in a fire had consumed her. She tried to pull herself together and stop the flames. Freezing in her tracks, she spotted a large garden hose propped against the house. *You've got to do this!* She untangled the yards of serpentine rubber hose and ran to turn on the nozzle.

As the flames trickled up to the second-floor bedrooms, a little furry face popped up in the window, "Willow!" Brittany threw the water hose to Blake and ran into the smoke-filled house. She lowered onto her knees and crawled as quickly as possible to the staircase, where she stood up again and ran to Macy's room. The dog was lying on the bed, panting, her eyes watering from smoke exposure. Brittany picked up Blake's faithful sidekick, scooting along the floor of her niece's bedroom while trying to avoid the pointy ends of hard plastic doll shoes and connective building blocks.

When they reached the staircase, Brittany picked up the trembling dog and ran down the steps. Unable to see more than a few feet in front of her, she hit the hardwood floor in the living room a little harder than expected, screaming but shaking off the pain. With the amount of smoke increasing, there was no time to assess injuries right now. Instead, she made a beeline for the front door. *Thank God I know this place like the back of my hand.*

Grabbing a throw blanket off the sofa, she balled it up in her hand and opened the front door. *We made it!* Brittany allowed herself to lie down in the grass and clear her lungs for a moment while holding onto Willow for dear life. She wasn't about to let go of her sister's best friend. The poor dog struggled to leap out of her arms, clearly concerned about her people. Brittany stroked her head. "Just a minute, girl, I've got to catch my breath. Then, I promise, I'll get you back to your family."

Clint ran up to Brittany, and she sat straight up, firing off questions. "How bad is the damage? Can we fix everything? Did we lose a lot?"

"Britt, are you crazy? That's all just stuff. First, tell me how you're doing. Are you breathing okay? Does anything hurt?"

"Nope. I'm alright. I just needed a sec to breathe in the fresh air. I'm good now."

"If you're sure, we need you in the garden right now," Clint said.

Brittany's jaw dropped. "So, it's pretty bad? Did we lose the kitchen?" She fought back the tears, thinking about all the mementos they may have lost.

"Nothing like that. We put out the fire. We'll definitely have some smoke damage, but the fire didn't destroy anything. There's a situation Blake needs your help to diffuse." He held out his hand for Brittany and pulled her up off the ground. Willow barked and followed them as they ran to join the fight.

Brittany couldn't have prepared for seeing Serena and Parker swinging at each other, a la the 1920s Golden Age of Boxing, on top of the cottage roof. Maggie jumped around, yelling obscenities at Serena every time she punched Parker. Brittany was unsure whether she should laugh or scream about the potential outcomes of this fight. She caught Blake's eye and signed, "What is wrong with them?"

Her sister shrugged. "They both randomly went bonkers. It's been hard to watch, especially while maintaining a straight face."

"I know, right? I should break it up so we can start." Brittany edged closer to the roof and looked up at Parker. "Hey, y'all gonna come down here so we can get all this squared away? None of us are getting any younger here."

Serena squatted, locking eyes with Brittany. "Yeah, we've, like, totally got a big score to settle." Serena rubbed her hands together, and the corners of her mouth pulled back into a smile. "So, who did you promise me?" Brittany motioned to come closer. Serena did a backward flip off the roof, landing just three feet from her. "So, like tell me already."

"How would you like to have twins?" Brittany smiled.

"Sounds like I'll have my hands full." Serena laughed. "But in a good way. So, do you have something we can use to bottle them?"

Brittany nodded. "I have the perfect idea." She drew a deep breath and ran toward Parker. "Here goes!"

Nancy cut her off, grabbing her hand. "Dear, are you sure you know what you're doing?"

"I've got this, Nancy." Brittany locked her gaze with her overprotective friend until she let go of her hand and gestured for her to go ahead.

The moment of truth had arrived. Would Brittany's plan work, or would Parker do something stupid like try to burn down the cottage for real? *There's no turning back, not when there's hell for someone, scratch that—two someones—to pay.*

Approaching Parker, she held her shoulders high, marching to the beat of her grandmother's song. The music fueled the adrenaline rush that pulsated through her body. She pulled the shell out of her pocket and held it up in the air for everyone to see. "I know you trapped my grandmother in here. Now, you need to release her. I'm tired of playing these games with you. Just tell the truth for once and do the right thing. Granny might take it easy on you if you do."

Parker spun out of control, grabbing Brittany by the shirt collar but holding her at arm's length so she could read his lips. "I told you. I didn't do it. I don't care anything about your grandma. I only wanted the shell because that sea witch over there wanted it so badly. I have no idea what she could even get out of having your grandmother trapped in there. What did your granny do to deserve that—steal their sea kelp?"

"You're such an asshole. If I have to hear that lie one more…" Brittany started, but before she could finish, Serena stormed her way over to where they stood. A breeze encapsulated Serena's body, blowing her hair upward. Her gray eyes had turned to an icy ocean blue.

"Why do you think he was the one who captured Julia Caroline?" Serena asked. "Alone, he's nothing. He needs his sister to amount to much of anything at all. Sure, he can turn some cute parlor tricks, but it's the power of being a twin that's helped him accomplish all of his more impressive work."

Brittany arched her eyebrow. "So, he and Maggie did it together. Same difference. He's still lying, so what does it matter if he did it on his own or with her? They're both nuisances, just like Palmetto bugs. I'm not a fan of squishing them; it's too much of a mess. But trapping them, that's a whole different story."

Serena laughed, but her smile faded. "What if I told you neither of them bottled your grandmother? It was me."

"But why would you do that?" Brittany asked. "What do you have to gain out of having Granny Mason? From what I read, someone who's been dead for more than ten years doesn't have much power on their own while bottled."

"I needed collateral to make sure I got what I wanted, which, I admit, was you, until I figured out who you were offering in exchange. Twins are the most powerful option, hence the reason for the oyster shell. It's an identical pair of shells that make a hospitable home for the spirits. It gives me more bang for my buck. Now that I'll have twins entrapped, the world is my oyster, quite literally. Having the Suttons in my control will be four times the power of having a single individual in a normal bottle."

Brittany smacked her hands together. "Okay! Let's do this. Please let my granny go."

Serena shook her head. "Hold up. First things first, let's make sure these two yahoos can't get away." She waved her hands and mumbled some words that Brittany couldn't quite make out. Water flowed from her fingertips like strands of rope, wrapping themselves around Parker and pulling him into the grand fountain Clint had restored for Blake right before their wedding. Hand-like appendages held him underwater.

"Where do you think you're going?" Serena screamed at Maggie, who'd begun her ascension. The wispy strands of water reached up for her and delivered her to the fountain beside Parker. Water sloshed over the side and sprayed Brittany. She wasn't sure how it was possible since spirits don't have mass, but it didn't matter. At least for right now, the Suttons weren't going anywhere. For the first time in almost a month, Brittany could breathe without panicking about what would come next. Sure, Serena was a little unhinged herself, but she was ready to make a bargain. Something occurred to Brittany—why did Serena need her to make the swap? Brittany shivered, looking over her shoulder at the mermaid.

Serena gazed at her coolly. "You're wondering why I'm going to such great lengths to make this happen. I've tried to get these two together in one place ever since they started hanging around that old, dilapidated shack. They were rarely there together, so I had to devise a plan. You made it easy on me." She smiled. "I needed you to host this little shindig. Since you've been such a great hostess, I'll give you what you wanted. Take out the shell."

Chapter 27

Brittany took a deep breath, hoping for the best. Granny Mason had been such a key force in their lives, even after her death. This spell had to go off without a hitch. Pulling the oyster out of her pocket, she felt the ridges of the shell. Serena approached her and held out her long, slender hand. "May I?"

Gulping, Brittany handed it over. She prayed for her grandmother. Her family. Herself. Focusing on her breathing, she watched Serena wave her hand over the shell and begin chanting, "Free the soul from its cell; give it the freedom to roam; allow it to come back home." Nothing happened.

"Why isn't it working?" Brittany demanded.

Serena smirked. "I need a drop of your blood."

"Why? What for?"

"Just trust me. Your grandmother has been on the Other Side for decades," Serena paused. "We need some fresh blood from her loved ones to help bring her back to this world."

Brittany winced. "How much are we going to need?

Blake ran up with a knife. "I'll go first," Closing her eyes, she pricked her finger. "Do I just drop the blood right onto the shell?"

Serena nodded. "Totally. Go for it when you're ready." She held the shell up toward Blake, who squeezed drops of blood from her fingertip. A glow pulsated from the oyster's interior.

Brittany marveled over the progress. "It's starting to work. Okay, hand me the knife. I'll go next." She sliced a small gash into her hand, biting her lip. Turning her hand upside down, she placed her palm on top of the shell. Blood gushed out of the cut, covering her grandmother's small but breathtaking prison. The illumination intensified and steadied; the shell rocked as if the two halves were trying to pull themselves apart at the seams. Elaina grabbed the knife out of her hands, "I'll take it the rest of the way home." She jabbed her palm, and deep crimson droplets splashed across the top of the oyster. The sections finally parted, and a mist spiraled out of the mollusk's shimmering interior. A cloud hovered over the shell, swirling behind the rose bushes. The leaves flapped back and forth, and Granny Mason popped up, covered in petals.

The Nelson sisters ran to hug their grandmother. "You're back!" Brittany exclaimed, wiping a tear of joy from her eye.

"Great job, girls!" Granny Mason pulled them in for another hug but let them go so she could sign. "I don't trust Serena; stay on guard at all times. This nightmare may not be over yet. I'll pray for the best, but I'm realistic. Too many people have disappointed me in my lifetime and, well, my afterlife, too."

Brittany turned to Serena. "Now, what do we have to do to get the Sinister Suttons moved into their new home? I'll be more than happy to throw them a housewarming party, complete with a gift registry after they're locked up where they belong."

Serena's grin widened to reveal her pointed, almost fang-like teeth. "Where they're going, they won't need much of anything. Think of it as the original epic tiny house, which will live inside a great big ocean. Doesn't everyone want a water view from their living room?" She cackled. "Sorry. I couldn't help myself. Let's get started. I need your family to gather around the fountain and hold hands. The eclipse will be in totality in a few minutes, and we can use all the extra magic we can get right now." Strolling over to the fountain, she climbed in beside Parker and Maggie. The evil spirits lay silent, still being held down by their watery captors.

Blake turned to Clint. "Hey, can you go get my mom off the porch?"

Brittany smiled. Susan didn't have the gift of seeing spirits like her daughters, but there was no doubt she would do whatever it took to end the torment that the Sutton family had caused her daughters.

Granny Mason and Nancy started creating the circle, and the rest of the family joined them. Watching Parker writhe in pain was a little unsettling, even though he was anything but the victim in this scenario. *Am I feeling guilty for making him hurt? No, this is what he deserves! You're doing this for Blake. It's been a long time coming.*

As if she'd read Brittany's mind, Blake turned to Serena with wide eyes. "Is he hurting? I don't want to see that. I can't…I mean, he's caused all of us here a great deal of pain over the years, but I don't enjoy tormenting someone. I just want him to go away for good."

Serena rolled her eyes. "Gag me with a spoon. Don't be so lame. I've got to keep him under wraps somehow unless you'd like to change places with him. I'd be happy to take you instead. I know you're the oldest, so you probably harnessed your powers earlier than your sisters."

Blake frowned but silently retreated to her place in the circle and hung her head down toward the ground. Brittany fought the urge to hug her sister; it was easy to see Serena was growing impatient with her family. She didn't need to do anything else to make matters more contentious.

Holding the open shell in one hand, Serena closed her eyes and began reciting a spell similar but somehow different from the bottling one Brittany had read in Maggie's book. "Send this pair away to their cell; never to leave—never to roam; make this their hell; their forever home." The mermaid waved her hand over Maggie, whose body expanded and contorted before it transformed into a shimmering film that the shell sucked into its depths. Brittany gulped. No matter how much she despised a person, it was difficult for her to reconcile that this spell had ended Maggie's earthly presence. *Wait! Where did Parker go?* A twinge of guilt pulled at Brittany's heartstrings when she spotted Parker's location. His body hovered over the shell, swinging like a pendulum. Serena pointed to him and gestured toward the oyster. Parker's feet flew upward until he was lying flat as if someone were carrying him on a silver platter. He reached out toward Brittany, screaming, "Help me!" Inch by inch, his body vanished into the depths of the shell.

Brittany's stomach churned, and her knees buckled. They'd done the right thing to protect their family, so why did she feel sick? Wide-eyed, she approached the shell. "Is that it? Will we have to redo the spell every month when their time is up?"

"Nope. You're thinking of the temporary bottling spell. My magic is more foolproof than all of that hocus pocus B.S. Girl, the Suttons have found their new crash pad. Only I can call them back out to do my bidding. This is totally bonkers—I have twins! And a deviously powerful duo at that!" Serena stroked the shell before she placed it inside the fountain. "So, like, thanks for your help. I know Parker had caused your family quite enough grief over the years. That's why it pains me that I have to do this."

"What are you talking about?" Brittany pursed her lips, staring at Serena.

The mermaid threw back her head, laughing, her long auburn ringlets bouncing. "You'll get it in just a minute." She motioned to one of her cronies to come over. "Heather, babe, can you take Brittany back home?"

"I am home; I don't get it," Brittany said. "I upheld my end of the bargain. What else do you want from me?" She let out a guttural scream. Her entire family ran to her side.

Susan grabbed Brittany's shoulder and signed, "What's wrong, honey? Is there something I can do? Just because I can't talk to the spirits doesn't mean I won't fight however

147

you need me to. I love you very much."

"Serena's trying to kill me!" Brittany cried.

Clint stepped up. "We won't let that happen. We've got your back 100 percent."

Granny Mason nodded in agreement. "Child, we could use the cleansing ceremony to send your mermaid nemesis to her final resting place instead, but we don't have much longer. The eclipse will vanish over the next hour. Can you create a diversion?"

Brittany saw Serena's eyes move from Granny to something else…Ryan was standing a few feet away! "What are you doing here? Shouldn't you be in the hospital resting? Are you strong enough to fight?"

He turned to her and signed, "I'll distract them. You've been through enough, and I can't let you take any more chances. What would I do if something happened to you? You've had too many close calls. It's my turn to help you."

"Don't—" Brittany started.

He shook his head, holding his finger to his lips to silence her. "You won't change my mind." He turned to talk to Julia Caroline. Brittany couldn't read his lips. And her grandmother wasn't speaking, just nodding occasionally. Typically, Ryan included Brittany in conversations. What was he keeping from her?

Chapter 28

Brittany couldn't take not knowing what Ryan was saying any longer. She stepped in front of him. "Hey, it's not cool for you to hide something from me. Don't I deserve to know what you're planning?"

Ryan shrugged. "You'll find out soon. Do me a huge favor and try not to worry, okay, babe?" He placed his hands onto her shoulders and gave them a slight squeeze.

Brittany bit her lip unintentionally, and blood began trickling down her chin. "I'm not okay with this situation at all, but what do you need?" Didn't he realize the mermaids could end his life along with the rest of the family's in a heartbeat?

"Be careful! You're hurting yourself." He pulled a tissue out of his pocket and applied pressure to her mouth. "Nancy and Elaina are going with me, and she's going to send a message to Granny Mason. I need you to stay here with Blake until your grandmother tells you it's time to help. Do you understand?"

"No. I don't want—" Brittany started, but a sticky lump formed in her throat, and tears spilled down her cheek. "I should go with you. You might need my help."

Ryan hugged her and kissed her forehead. "I love you." His eyes widened as he turned to Nancy, who simply nodded. Running in one swift motion, he grabbed the oyster shell from the fountain, put it into his pocket and jumped into his truck. Nancy and Elaina climbed in, too, and they sped away down Palm Court.

Did Serena see that? Surely not, or she would have drowned him and Elaina with her deadly aqueous hands. Who knows what she would have done to Nancy since she was already dead? Brittany drew a deep breath and looked over at Serena, who was busily chatting with her groupies. Hopefully, she wouldn't notice that the shell or that a few of her family members were missing. They needed a head start.

Breathe in, breathe out. It will all be okay. Ryan is smart, and he has Nancy and Elaina with him. So, why did this whole diversion plan make her feel like throwing up?

Serena left her merfolk, making a beeline for Brittany. *Great! Just great! Here we go!* The sea witch, as Parker had called her, stood eye to eye with Brittany. Stepping back a few paces, she flashed an unnatural smile. "So, like, what are we going to do with you? I want to keep that boyfriend of yours, too. I'm gaga for that butt of his. A strategically placed starfish is all he'll need to wear once we're back in the water."

Brittany clenched her fists, digging her fingernails into her hand. "Why are you doing this?" She should have known better than to trust this witch.

"You'll, like, make sure no one tries to upend our posh underwater lifestyle. It took some getting used to, but now, I'm quite partial to it. Some people, mostly dead people, want to destroy what we have. Your powers will come in handy when we need to send those bitches away to their next destination. I don't want to bottle up useless creatures every time I turn around."

"But why do you want Ryan? He has no magical abilities, well, except for being able to see you since he loves me."

Serena giggled. "I thought I'd made that clear. He's a piece of magical, sexy eye candy, and I may be dead now, but I used to be a red-blooded woman with needs. Let's just say he might come in handy if the mood strikes."

"He'd never sleep with a blobfish like you, whore," Brittany muttered under her breath.

150

"What did you say?" Serena's eyes narrowed and glowed red. "Do you want to die right now? I was going to give you and Mr. Handsome some time alone, one last hurrah before my crew drugged and drowned you. It would have been a peaceful way to go, but now, I'm ready to slit your throat with a chunk of fire coral and throw you to the sharks that circle the pier. Hey, where is he anyway? I know I've been distracted, but how did he sneak away?"

Brittany shrugged and stared blankly at Serena. Did the sea witch actually think Brittany would help her?

"Tsk. Tsk. You'd better keep a closer eye on your man if you don't want him to slip through your fingers. Although it won't matter for long because literally, everything slips through your fingers when you're dead." Serena motioned to two of her followers to come over, and when they were a few feet away, she started barking orders. "Ethan—watch this one. It looks like lover boy has disappeared. He couldn't have gotten too far. I don't want her texting him or nothin' like that. Lollie, you need to go after him. I trust you don't need me to spell out the most common places you might find him."

Ethan grabbed Brittany's hand, pulling her over to the fountain. "Get in." She looked at him incredulously and shook her head.

"I said, 'Get into the damn fountain, now!" Ethan yelled.

Brittany stepped into the fountain and curtsied. "Happy?"

"Don't sass me. I'm not afraid to take down a bitch, regardless of how important she thinks she is."

She put her hand on her hip and looked at him out of the corner of her eye. "Me either."

"Whatever, just sit down and don't make a peep; got it?"

She sat down and folded her legs underneath her. Granny Mason caught her eye and signed, "Be patient. We should hear from Nancy soon."

On that note, Susan, Blake and Clint moved closer to the fountain, but not so close as to agitate Serena or Ethan. Blake stared at Brittany. "Are you okay? Did he hurt you?"

"No. I'm just wet and a little cold, but I'll survive," Brittany signed with a smirk. "How has she not noticed that the shell is missing?"

"I don't know, but I'm so grateful. Hopefully, they can put a lot of road in between them and Lollie. I heard her talking to Serena. When she was alive, she did time in prison for hunting down people for the mob."

Brittany gulped and buried her head in her hands. This is crazy. *Why did I let him go?* He shouldn't be part of this. Ryan had left, but that didn't mean she wouldn't worry. He was strong; nothing has kept him down. Nancy and Elaina won't let anything happen to him. *He's probably safer on the road than being here right now.* Brittany looked upward. The eclipse had faded even more. "Hey, Granny, come here."

Granny Mason nodded toward Serena and her henchmen. She signed, "Wait a minute." When the mermaids huddled together, she scooted in closer. "Okay, somehow Ryan's theft has gone unnoticed. Thank God for small favors. Let's go old school and hold a cleansing ceremony."

"But Serena banished Parker and Maggie to the oyster shell," Brittany said.

"Yes, but Serena and her friends haven't been. We've gotta send them along to their next stop." Granny Mason winked.

"That could work, but we don't have personal effects for all these people." Brittany winced. "We might manage it for Serena, but she'd be the only one."

"Apparently, you didn't read Chapter 20 of my book," Granny Mason said.

"No." Brittany looked at Blake, who shrugged. "Everything we needed to deal with Parker was in Chapter 19, so we didn't bother reading much further."

Granny Mason peered over her glasses. "Well, girls, you need to be a little more thorough when fighting evil spirits. You can never have too much information. Now, let's get started. Blake, can you slip away and gather a few things?"

They walked off together, and Brittany couldn't read their lips. But her grandmother could pull off just about anything.

Chapter 29

Blake emerged from the front yard, motioning for Brittany to come over, but she shook her head, pointing to Ethan, who stood a few feet away.

"Come on. We're running out of time before the mermaids' time on land expires. Granny said we've gotta get a move on right now. Figure out a way to get up for a minute without them noticing."

Brittany jumped up and clutched her stomach, "Ethan, I'm about to be sick!"

"So? Throw up over in the bushes or whatever, just leave me alone."

Doubled over, Brittany shook her head. "Not that way. I need a bathroom right now. I'm cramping badly. I've got to take some medicine and drink some ginger ale, or else we're going to have a disaster zone out here."

He scowled. "Fine. Go on, but come straight back out here, and use the back door. I'm sending someone to guard the front door, so you can't try to sneak out that way."

Nodding, she threw him a peace sign and ran inside. Feeling her way through the thick smoke, Brittany settled in the downstairs bathroom. Thankfully, little smoke had seeped into the rooms since both doors had been closed. A few minutes later, Blake and Granny Mason joined her. "You're not really sick, right?" Blake asked.

"No, of course not. I just needed a convenient excuse to get away so we could talk."

Granny Mason shushed them, putting her index finger to her lips. "Girls, I've got an idea that's so crazy it might work. What's the one thing these mermaids are most afraid of?" Her eyes twinkled. "I don't think you saw their reaction to Parker's pyrotechnics earlier. They ran around like chickens with their heads cut off. Obviously, dying in the hotel fire still haunts them. We should build on that and show them some more fireworks they won't forget."

Brittany smirked. "Why don't y'all slip away and get the show ready? For whatever reason, they're not paying attention to you guys."

"Yep. You'd better get back outside, or the mermaids are going to get suspicious. Don't forget to look at least a little green when you go back out there. Give us a head start." Blake left the room. Brittany counted to 100 and walked to the garden.

"It took you long enough," Ethan said through his gritted teeth. "You look pretty rotten, though. I thought you might have died. It would have been a real shame, too. I'm looking forward to watching the life drain right out of you when Serena kills you."

"Glad I didn't disappoint you." Brittany flipped him off and stuck out her tongue. Sure, it was immature, but she didn't care. He was getting on her last nerve, and crude gestures most commonly used by preteen boys were the best she had at the moment.

Ethan held his hand up if he were planning to slap her. "Shut your mouth and get back into the fountain."

As Blake and Clint slipped out the garden gate, Brittany stepped into the water. Her teeth chattered, but there was no point in complaining. She settled into the fountain, relaxing her muscles and focusing on breathing. What were her sister and brother-in-law doing? They were such a perfect match, and Clint hadn't left Blake throughout Parker's hauntings. Now, he was about to help their family take down the mermaids. Ryan had proven his devotion as well, running off with the shell. As far as Brittany knew, Serena still hadn't noticed that the shell was missing. What could she possibly be cooking up that she'd missed such a huge detail?

Brittany's heart pounded in her throat. Cold chills crept down her extremities, and her breathing turned erratic. She couldn't have a panic attack right now. It had been eight years since the last one. Drawing a deep breath, she closed her eyes for just a moment and forced herself to think about something positive. Naturally, marrying Ryan was the first thing to come to mind.

They'd committed to each other at such a young age that she barely remembered life without him, not that she wanted that to change. More than anything, she wanted to start their lives together, including their careers. She took comfort in knowing that every day, when she came home from work, he'd be there, too. That guarantee was better than any expensive gift or grandiose gesture that many young women expected from their partners. The best part of their relationship is that he never treated her like she had a disability or limitations. He often described her attitude about her hearing impairment as just another reason to love her— she'd never let being deaf defeat her. And, damn it, that wasn't about to change now.

Opening her eyes, she squinted. Fire danced along the roofline and threatened to climb down the trellis on the house's backside, consuming the whole cottage. Even though she knew the flames were a mirage, cooked up by her granny, her stomach lurched when they spread to the house's interior, promising to cremate her family's childhood memories, mementos, not to mention everyday possessions. *This isn't real. Just breathe. The house is okay, and so are you.*

Scanning the garden for her family, she hadn't expected to find Clint and Blake hiding behind a rose bush with Willow, snickering. *What was so funny?* Across the yard, Serena and several of her followers ran around with their bodies engulfed in flames. They hopped around, screaming and occasionally bumping into each other. The sight was pretty hilarious. Getting Blake's attention, Brittany signed, "Why haven't they figured out the fire isn't real?"

"They can't sense heat, but the memory of the hotel fire is pretty traumatic. If this were any other group of people, I'd feel more sympathetic. For now, we're just messing with them to run out the clock. They've only got half an hour left before they turn back into fish, pumpkins or whatever the mermaids are when they live in the water."

Brittany laughed. "Well, I'll go make some popcorn so we can sit back and enjoy the show." But when she saw the sheer panic on Serena's face, she stopped laughing. Red and blue flames swaddled the mermaid from head to toe. Somehow, the fire accentuated her natural beauty, but the pained expression on her face made Brittany's heart ache. She couldn't stop the illusion without risking her family's well-being, but that didn't mean it was the right thing to do. "Granny, isn't there another way? I hate to torture anyone like this. We've been on the receiving end of absolute terror, off and on for years. I want to keep them off our backs, but at what price?"

Granny Mason chewed her cheek. "Just the cleansing ceremony or the basic bottling spell, but I don't like either of those options. I haven't ever needed to banish underwater dwelling spirits. This is an odd situation, to say the very least. They're the first aqueous specters I've had the displeasure of meeting, and I wouldn't have gotten to know them except that I've been friends with Lorna since she was a child. She asked me to watch over Jenny as much as possible. Their underwater lair isn't easy to get into. Guards line the entrance, and even if you can get past them, it's like a maze. It took me at least a dozen visits to get used to the flow of all the chambers."

"Gah... yeah. let me think about it for a minute." As she ran through a gamut of ideas, Brittany wrestled with her voluminous hair and pulled the tangled waves back into a ponytail. Should they try the cleansing ceremony? It hadn't worked out so well with Parker; they'd ended up with double trouble instead, with Maggie adding to the mix. Brittany would be glad if she never met twins, especially dead ones, again. Their supernatural abilities outweighed any other spirit paired with another. *Stop getting off track. You need to be thinking about how to get rid of the mermaids.* Granny Mason had brought up a good point when she asked what mermaids hated the most—something that would bring a definite, quick end to the mermaids' time on earth and a sense of peace and finality for the Nelson family.

Brittany punched her palm. "I've got it. We have to get back over to Sweetgrass Island right now. Clint, can you stay behind and watch to make sure they disappear in about an hour and text Blake if anything goes wrong?" He nodded, and she fist-bumped him before taking one last look at the mermaids, who showed no signs of noticing their time was almost up. Brittany waved to get the rest of her family's attention. "C'mon, we've gotta get to the marina, stat."

Chapter 30

Weaving through the tidal creeks in Clint's boat, the earthy scent of pluff mud filled the air. Some people couldn't stand the odor, but the marsh smelled like Brittany's childhood summers on the island. Part of her hair slipped out of the bun and flew up over her face. She pushed it out of the way and secured the long, loose strands while steering the boat with her other hand.

Sweetgrass Island was just ahead. Brittany drew a deep breath and prepared to tie off the boat outside the Sutton's shack. She stood back and checked her work—not too shabby. It'd been a hot minute since she'd needed to tie a nautical knot. Thankfully, Granny Mason's sailing lessons had resonated, sticking to her brain like flies in molasses.

As Granny Mason stepped off the boat, she nodded in approval. "Beautiful work, Britt. Now, let's get ready for these floundering spirits to return to their watery grave." Brittany's mom and sisters followed them to the seagrass covered bank.

Susan turned to Brittany. "So, what's next?"

"We just need to wait for our special guest." Brittany smiled.

"Who's that?" Blake asked. "Do you have some sort of magical army coming to save us?"

"Let's just say she's a fighter, but she shouldn't need to fight too hard today." Brittany grinned. "Everything should go swimmingly." She winked.

Water sloshed over the edge of the dock, soaking

Brittany's shoes. Her feet squished with every step. Cringing, she looked around, trying to find the source of the splash, but, suddenly, the wooden boards shook underneath her feet. Something rammed the supports, causing Brittany to lose her balance and fall into the water. A large sandpaper-like textured object brushed up against her back. She shuddered and tried to will the coldness away from her body. In the darkness, she reached out for something, anything or anyone, to get out of the icy water. Turning around, she was face to face with a glowing set of eyes. If they belonged to her guest of honor, a punch square in the nose should do the trick. She drew a deep breath, reared back and launched her fist toward the shark's face. The massive fish retreated and floated in stillness. Suddenly, someone pulled Brittany up by her shirt. She flew through the air, landing on her back. The impact knocked the wind out of her, but she was out of the water.

Blake stood over her, moving her hands at a furious pace. "What on earth? Are you okay? Was that an effing shark? In the Intracoastal? How did that happen?"

"Bull sharks can go back and forth between saltwater and freshwater—" Brittany started.

"How do you know that?" Blake asked. "Never mind, but how did it get here?"

Brittany shrugged. "Well, I may have attached a chum bucket to the bottom of the boat before we left the marina."

"Are you insane? Do you want us to die?"

"Of course not, but if we don't deal with Serena and her deranged crew, they're going to kill us. At some point, you have to choose the lesser of two evils, and right now, I'd rather face a shark than a mermaid, if that means we can put this paranormal business behind us for good."

Blake nodded, biting her lip. "Only about 20 minutes until the mermaids have to return home. What do we need to do?"

Brittany handed Blake her phone. "Study the bottling spell. It's unconventional, but we have to try it. After all,

Serena trapped Parker and Maggie in an oyster shell. Why would a shark be any different?"

Blake's jaw dropped. "You've got to be kidding me. This is your great idea? They'll be here any minute, and we're not sure if this hair-brained plan will work?"

"We're running out of options." Brittany shrugged. "Go read and pass the phone around to everyone else so they can catch up to speed."

Blake didn't move, so Brittany read the screenshot of Maggie's spell book and took it to Susan.

Granny Mason must have seen Blake's forlorn expression. She floated across the water to where the sisters stood and rubbed her arm. "It's going to be okay, child. You've lived through all of this before, and you came out stronger for it. Don't forget your family stood by you through everything with Parker. He was your fiancé, but Brittany was right there to defend you the whole time. She still is." Granny Mason patted Blake's hand and walked away.

Blake looked up at Brittany. "She's right. You wouldn't be in this whole mess if it weren't for my bad life choices. If I hadn't ever dated Parker, we'd all be safer, healthier and happier. He's cost us many opportunities for peace and success while we've had to right all of his wrongs." Blake paused and inhaled a deep breath. As she exhaled, she signed. "I'll do whatever you need me to do. I love you."

"Thanks, sis. Just get ready. We're not magicians or witches or whatever, so I hope this works. I guess it's kind of like baking when you're not a baker or a chef. At least we have a recipe that we know works. Fake it until you bake, uh, make it."

Blake smiled weakly. "You're so strong. I can't believe that you're not sweating bullets right now. How are you keeping your cool?"

"Breathing, praying and adrenaline. That's all I've got going for me right now. Stay calm. God will get us through this. I'm sure of it. He has brought us this far, and I'm sure there's a reason for that. There has to be."

Blake paced the yard until a golden light shimmered across the water. She stopped in her tracks and looked at Brittany, who turned to Granny Mason.

"Okay, girls. They're almost back. Get ready to recite the incantation."

"Wait!" Brittany yelled. "What about Jenny? Is she going to be okay?"

"Don't worry. I took care of Jenny. She'll be fine. I'll tell you later. We've got to get started."

Susan pulled her daughters into a circle along the bank. They huddled in close, taking each other's hands and watching for Granny Mason to give them the signal to begin. A cold blast of wind chilled Brittany to the core. Shivering, she signed, "They're back. I can just feel it." She looked back to her grandmother for confirmation, and the second she signed, "Now!" the Nelson women began chanting, "Send these spirits to their cell, never again to roam the earth, Heaven or Hell. End their torment and their haunting; let the fear of them only be a memory, one less daunting."

The mermaids had vanished. Did that mean the spell had worked? Brittany peered over the bank's edge, staring at the shark which was gliding through the water.

Granny Mason scrunched her nose. "I'm not looking forward to going down there, but I want to make sure *everything* took hold as planned. I'll be right back."

"I saw Clint's diving tank in the boat. I'm going with you." Brittany grabbed the tank and some other gear, thankful her dad had insisted that their family maintain diver certifications over the years. He always said, "You never know when you might need or want to dive." She'd always laughed at him, but it turned out he was right.

"Hon, I've got this," Granny Mason signed. "You don't have to go with me."

"I know, but Jenny is my friend. I want to make sure she's safe and see with my own two eyes that we've locked away those demented mermaids for good." She bit her lip.

"What happens to them if someone catches the shark, or if it dies of old age? Will they be able to escape? Can they possess the shark somehow?"

"Heavens, no, child. The shark will pass the spirits on to its offspring, and the cycle will continue forever. And the mermaids aren't able to possess anyone or anything. Now, I really must go to investigate their lair. I don't want any surprises."

Brittany suited up and jumped into the water. Even wearing a wet suit, it took a minute to acclimate. She forgot about her discomfort once she saw the scene before her. Growing up in Tennessee, she had dived in rivers plenty of times, but not an Atlantic estuary. Oysters clung to every rocky surface; vibrant seagrass and fish swayed to the rhythm of the flowing water. Catching up with Granny Mason, Brittany watched her pause at the cavern entrance, which had formed where two boat ramp footings had collapsed. Waving her hand, Granny Mason moved a massive boulder aside as if it were a small pebble.

Brittany followed her into the room, which glowed with the iridescence of mother-of-pearl. Her grandmother picked up a pink and red scallop shell and examined it before placing it into her pocket. "Jenny is safe. Sometimes, we can use the bottling spell for a good purpose. This way, Lorna can protect her daughter, and they can be together any time they want. Now, for the potentially unpleasant part. Stay on guard." A whirlpool formed, picking up sediment and clumps of seaweed in its swirling force. Brittany braced herself for whatever came next, tempted to close her eyes, but she thought better of it.

A cold blast of water pummeled her body, and she turned to see the shark swimming in their direction at full speed. Brittany clenched her jaw as much as she could with the regulator in her mouth. Steadying her breathing, she watched in terror as the fish made a beeline for them. When it was a mere five feet away, the whirlpool pulled its tail into the rotation, and it spun in circles directly in front of Brittany.

163

Finally, the vortex moved like a tornado or a waterspout, carrying the shark to the other side of the cavern room. Granny Mason motioned for her to leave. "Let's go quickly now!" Brittany swam at a quick and steady pace, stopping outside the cavern. Her grandmother waved her hand once again, covering the cavern door. "Alright, it's time for you to get out of the water. I don't want you to cut it too close with your oxygen tank. I'll be back up in a minute."

Ascending to the surface, Brittany reflected on everything that had happened since she'd moved to South Carolina. Two short weeks here had seemed like an eternity. Things had to get better now that the Nelson sisters and their grandmother had locked Parker, Maggie and the mermaids in their prisons. She couldn't wait to see Ryan and find out about the adventure he and Nancy had taken to help safeguard their family. One thing's for sure; they'd never had a boring life.

Chapter 31

Astillness filled the air, hopefully, a sign that the evil forces hellbent on destroying the Nelson family had finally left the world for good. Brittany and her family could use a reprieve from torture, sadness, stress. What a strange thought…a life without pain inflicted by evil spirits. Could it be possible?

Underneath Brittany's feet, the earth shook. *Great. I jinxed myself. Here comes the next big bad.* She held her breath, half-closed her eyes and doubled over in laughter when Granny Mason emerged from the water with a spark of light. "You scared me to death!"

Granny Mason brushed a sliver of slimy seagrass off her arm. "Sorry, hon. I didn't mean to take so long, but I wanted to check in on our *friends*. I'll visit them now and then, just to make sure they don't get any funny ideas."

"Did we do the right thing using the bottling spell instead of trying the cleansing ceremony again? I mean, we sent Parker on to his next destination. We just didn't realize how much Maggie looked like him or how conniving she could be. I think the spell was a good bet for locking up the Sinister Suttons, but the mermaids know the bottling incantations like the back of their proverbial fins. Should we be worried they might undo it themselves or communicate with someone who can help them?"

"No, child. We can't worry about such things. Staying positive is half the battle. Spirits can smell fear. There's always a risk, regardless of what method you used to rid yourself of a hitchhiking spirit. That's why I locked them in the cavern. There's a colony of sharks that live in there, plus a slew of fish for them to feed on. The shark can still thrive—eat and produce offspring. It just can't roam the ocean from one end to the next."

Brittany nodded. Her grandmother knew more about getting rid of spirits than most people knew about themselves. The brilliant woman had written her book about banishing ghosts in the 1960s when many didn't accept the paranormal subject matter. Granny Mason had helped many people get rid of malevolent and sometimes dangerous spirits during her extraordinary life. In death, she'd refused to cross over to the Other Side, so she could continue serving others during extreme hauntings. No one had ever questioned Granny Mason's fundamental mission—to protect her family above all else. Her opinion and beliefs meant everything to Brittany. If she said they were safe, it was so.

Inhaling the salty marsh air, a sense of renewal and positivity overcame Brittany. She sat on the dock and lay on the weathered boards, allowing the sun's rays to caress her sore and tired body. A light breeze cooled the temperature ever so slightly, and she relaxed, becoming one with her environment. The intoxicating sensation of teetering on the edge of sleep calmed her soul, and she slipped off to dreamland, where images of Ryan and a beautiful baby—their baby—cuddled on an overstuffed couch in a light-filled room. Her heart swelled…what a great, loving Dad! Just as quickly as the dream had begun, it faded, turning to darkness, except for an ominous set of narrowed green eyes.

A tap on her shoulder woke her. Covered in sweat, she jumped to her feet, fists at her side. "Who's there? What do you want?"

She spun around to see Ryan holding a bottle of her favorite sports drink and a pizza box. "Oh, my God! I was so worried about you and Nancy. What happened?"

"We're fine, and most importantly, Parker and Maggie won't be messing with you or your family again. Nancy and her friend, I think her name was Paulene, made sure of that. We drove three hours away to the middle of nowhere and dug a hole into the side of a mountain. No one's ever going to find that shell. And even if they did, Nancy, Paulene and Elaina chanted something in Latin before we buried it. They swear it's impenetrable. Anyone who stumbled across it would think it was just a seashell that someone accidentally dropped in the mountains. By the way, Paulene has an interesting sense of style."

Brittany laughed while imagining the aging woman who wore boldly colored dresses or suits, accentuated by crystal pendants or broaches. "She does, but she is a kind woman who has helped us out of several pinches over the years. We're lucky to have her on our side."

"Amen to that." Ryan smiled and handed her the pizza box. "Eat up. I hope it's not too cold."

Brittany noticed the branding on the box—Luke and Ollie's. Taking her first bite of a slice, she remembered that their pizza had something special about it. Maybe the pizzeria's secret ingredient was geography. After all, doesn't everything taste better by the beach?

Ryan smiled at her. "I'm glad I could help you. Having lived so far apart, I haven't had the chance to take care of you the way I've wanted. From here on out, I promise to be here for you. You know I'd do anything for you, right?"

"Same. Always." Brittany led him into the shack, locking the door behind her. "Let's take care of each other right now." She pulled off her clothes, followed by his. As she kissed every inch of Ryan's body, his chest heaved in time with her touch. He picked her up and took her to the sofa, where they made love for hours.

Coming up for air, Brittany realized she'd forgotten about her family. She dressed quickly and ran outside. Warm fat raindrops splotched as they hit puddles across the yard. Where had her family taken cover during the storm? She looked around but didn't see any sign of them or Clint's boat. Ugh, they must have left.

Ryan ran outside with her cell phone in hand. "Hey babe, your family went back home." He raised his eyebrow. "Um, they didn't want to disturb us earlier. Clint will come to pick us up if you're ready."

"Please ask him to come now." Brittany folded her arms over her chest. She couldn't blame her family for wanting to get the heck out of Dodge, but how could they abandon her in the very place where Parker and Maggie had held her captive? Sure, it would have interrupted their special moment, but they should have knocked on the door for Ryan to hear, called one of their phones or found another way to make contact before up and leaving them without a boat to return to Isle of Palms.

"Are you okay?" He massaged her shoulders.

"Yeah, I'm just a little pissed off that my family left us here without telling us they were going to, but I'll get over it. I guess I understand why they did."

Ryan lifted her chin with his index finger and kissed her pout. "I'm glad they gave us some space and me a chance to reconnect with the woman I'm marrying today."

Brittany's mouth gaped. "We're still getting married today? You know we don't have to rush it now that we didn't follow the cleansing ceremony. It would be nice to have at least a month to pull everything together. I don't even have a dress. And what about your family? Could they even get here in time?"

He dropped to his knee and held her hand. "Brittany—" He never called her anything but *Babe* or *Britt*, so he had her full attention. "I don't care about having the perfect clothing, guest list or flowers. All I need for our wedding is you. But why don't we just push the wedding to tomorrow so we can get some rest?"

She kissed Ryan gently. Lights flashing from the water caught her attention. Clint's boat was sitting at the dock where Clint and her dad were clapping and cheering. Brittany's cheeks reddened. "Gosh, Clint, now that you have a kid, I guess you can be just as corny as our dad."

Clint winked. "That's how it works. Ryan will be the same way when y'all have some little ones."

"Gee, I look forward to that." Brittany rolled her eyes but smiled, thinking about her dream about Ryan and their baby. She realized her period was almost two weeks late. *It's probably nothing—stress can cause issues with my cycle. I won't worry about it for a few more days, but what if I'm pregnant? When could I have conceived? Was it during his coma? No, it couldn't be, but what if?*

"What are you thinking about?" Ryan kissed her on the forehead.

"Nothing, or at least I think it's nothing…" Brittany started. "But it could be something." She grinned. "You'll be the first to know. I promise."

Chapter 32

As Brittany opened the front door to the cottage, she expected a cloud of smoke to assault her. Instead, a slight haze and a tinge of odor filled the air. When Susan walked down the stairs, Brittany ran to hug her. "How on earth did you guys get rid of the smoke? I figured the damage would be devastating."

"One of Clint's friends from the fire department knew someone with specialized equipment for removing smoke from an older home. I guess it helps to live so close to Charleston, where they know about these things. But, honey, let's talk about what matters. I'm so relieved you're okay."

"I'm glad we all survived another crazy haunting, to put it mildly. All I want now is to live a normal-ish life—get married, figure out where we're going to live and start my career."

"And have a baby?" Susan's eyes twinkled.

Brittany stared at her mother. How did she know? Brittany wasn't even sure herself. A missed period and a dream about a baby were no guarantee.

"You girls may have inherited my mom's abilities to see and communicate with the dead, but I have her sixth sense about telling if someone is pregnant or lying. I don't know how those two things belong together, but they're part of who I am."

Brittany's eyes widened. "I never knew that about you."

"How do you think I caught you in all of those lies when you were a teenager?" Susan laughed. "It prevented you from making some horrible decisions."

"Lord, I think I'm going to be sick." Brittany feigned retching.

"Be careful. You may do that for real every morning for the next several months. I wouldn't tempt fate."

"Good point. I guess I should take a pregnancy test, but I want to wait until after the wedding. I don't want Ryan to find out until I'm sure."

"Of course, I can't wait to be a grandma again." Susan wiped a tear from her cheek. "Sorry for being emotional. You girls have been through so much. I'm so proud of all of you!"

Brittany was proud of her sisters, too. Elaina had just received a promotion at the bank where she worked, and the last time she and her boyfriend, Todd, had visited Atlanta, he'd asked Brittany what kind of engagement ring he should buy. Her wedding would be next.

Susan waved to get Brittany's attention again. "So, Ryan said you two are getting married tomorrow. Let's talk through everything."

Blake and Elaina walked into the room. "What are we talking about?" Elaina asked.

"My wedding is tomorrow, and I have nothing that I need to get married other than my family." Brittany cringed.

Blake put out her hand. "Stay right here. I can take care of almost everything for you over the next hour. Do you trust me to pick out everything?"

Brittany gave her a thumbs up. She couldn't afford to be picky in the short time frame, and her sister planned dozens of weddings every year at the bed and breakfast. Blake knew all the wedding vendors in the area. Springing into action, her sister ran into the garden, almost tackling their dad, who had just arrived. Brittany watched her talk to him, Clint and Ryan. Whatever she asked of them, they nodded furiously and climbed into Clint's Jeep.

Being the oldest, her sister knew how to take charge and not apologize for what she needed.

A cold breeze chilled Brittany as Blake ran back inside and upstairs without slowing down to talk to them again.

"She's a force to be reckoned with," Susan said. "It's a good thing that Clint is so easy going. Otherwise, their personalities would probably clash in a bad way."

Elaina giggled. "I wonder what she's got up her sleeve. I'll keep her in mind for a wedding planner when the time comes."

A knowing glance passed between Brittany and Susan, but thankfully, Elaina didn't seem to notice.

Blake ran back into the room, her arms loaded with dresses, shoes, flowers and random papers. "Okay, I think I've got this wedding planned!" She rattled off details about the marriage license, flowers from the garden, a cake, a photographer and the suits she'd sent the guys to pick up. Afterward, she handed Brittany a pile of dresses to rummage through.

Brittany drew a deep, restoring breath. "I'm a little overwhelmed. I'll just start trying on dresses, and you guys can tell me which one works best." The first one she came to was a high-low white strapless dress with pale yellow daisy accents. It was cute but more appropriate for a barbeque than a wedding. She tried on a few more fun numbers, but nothing clicked in the try-on process. Sticking out of the bottom of the stack of dresses, a champagne-hued, tea-length organza gown with three-quarter length lace sleeves called her name. Stepping into the dress, she twirled in the full skirt. A slight shimmer gave the material a glow without being obnoxiously glittery. "This one seems familiar. Did you wear it to a party?"

Granny Mason appeared in a silvery translucent film. "Hon, it's my wedding gown, and I'd be honored if you wore it. Y'all know how blessed Papa and I were during our marriage; we want that for all of you, too."

A single tear rolled down Brittany's cheek. "It's perfect, and I wouldn't want to wear any other dress." Granny Mason pulled her in for a tight embrace. Thank God for the short wedding planning time frame. If she'd had time to shop, Blake might not have thought to present the dress as an option. Instead, Brittany would have bought some overpriced dress at a bridal salon that had no back story or meaning to her family.

Blake dried her eyes. "I also brought you the veil and jewelry I wore at my wedding. If they're not your taste, you can rummage through my jewelry box."

"You've thought of everything, and I can't thank you enough. I'm so lucky to have you all in my life."

Susan walked up. "There's one more thing you're going to need tomorrow—rings. I'd like you to use my parents' wedding bands." She placed two gold bands into Brittany's hand. Intricate scrollwork adorned the edges, and each ring had the same inscription, *June 8, 1960: Now and always.* Her grandparents had the sweetest relationship and most passionate romance, the pure definition of life goals for each of the Nelson sisters.

Keeping her emotions in check was no easy feat right now...*yikes*...another sign of a potential pregnancy. *Don't get ahead of yourself. Relax. You'll know for sure tomorrow.* Even after giving herself a pep talk, she needed to take her mind off the situation at hand. A nap might do the trick. "Hey, I'm going to crash for an hour or so. I'm just a little overwhelmed, and I think it will help. Thanks again for helping me, everyone. Love y'all."

Chapter 33

When Brittany woke from her nap, the guys had just returned to the house with suit bags, a case of beer and a few white and green shopping bags, which were the source of a delicious aroma. She ran up to lend them a hand, snatching the shopping bags and taking a peek. "What do you have here?" Containers overflowing with fried seafood, biscuits, fried green tomatoes and grits sat inside each bag. "I'm drooling!"

Ryan smirked. "Clint said your family loves Page's Okra Grill, so we stopped there to get some seafood and dessert for everyone. I can't wait to dig in and try the food. I was tempted to steal a shrimp during the whole ride back to the cottage."

"The Lowcountry, especially the food, will get into your blood if you're not careful," Brittany teased.

"Would that be such a bad thing? I know you love it here." He was right. Blake's family lived in their family home, and there were plenty of job options in Charleston. They'd have built-in babysitters, and their kid could grow up with Macy. She'd have a few years on the kid, so she can show them the ropes and be a positive influence on them.

As if Ryan was reading her mind, he placed his hand on her stomach and smiled. Brittany's jaw dropped. "Wait…how do you know about the baby? Did my mom tell you? I shouldn't have told her, but she guessed."

"Nobody told me anything. I had a dream about holding a

baby the other night. I couldn't stop smiling even when I woke up. When I saw you a few minutes ago, I just knew. Somehow, you're even more beautiful now than earlier today. When do you think it happened?"

"I haven't taken a test yet. I'm hesitant to say it happened during my graduation weekend—you were in a coma. I can't explain how that would work." She held her stomach and smiled at Ryan. "I guess it's time to find out if we're having a baby."

Susan walked into the room, staring at them and grinning ear to ear. "Sounds like he knows." She wasn't surprised her mom had been eavesdropping. Her reaction to the possible pregnancy hadn't been exactly subtle.

Brittany nodded. "He had the same dream." She jumped up and down. "Gah…we can't wait until after the wedding to find out. We want to know for sure right now."

"I'll be right back." Susan ran upstairs and returned quickly with a small box in her hand. "I figured it was best to have it here when you were ready."

She's so impatient. Brittany giggled, taking the box from Susan and walking into the powder room. Placing the test stick on the sink, she walked out of the room. "Do anything to distract me for a few minutes."

Macy ran into the room. "Auntie Britt, I'm home! Hugs!" *Perfect timing!*

"Did you have fun with your cousins, kiddo?" Brittany asked as her niece hugged her leg.

The tot pulled away and signed, "So much fun! We went swimming and saw the prettiest mermaids."

"Where did you see mermaids?" Brittany stared at Blake, who shrugged, signing, "She has a wild imagination. Don't worry."

"At the beach. Mermaids in pretty outfits swam in circles. I love them. They my friends." Macy pretended to swim, adding a twirl and curtsy to the end of each stroke of her arms.

Brittany smiled weakly. "Honey, I'm so glad you're back.

175

Why don't you change out of your swimsuit?" As her niece danced up the steps to her room, Brittany locked eyes with Blake. "Can you call Clint's brother and see where he took the kids? If the mermaids are free, that's bad news for all of us."

"Yep, but don't forget the mermaids we know don't have fish tails or fins. She wouldn't know to call them mermaids." Blake picked up her phone and dialed Chris's number. "Hey, where did you take the kids swimming?"

After a few minutes, Blake ended the call and giggled. "He took them to the aquarium, and there was a woman dressed as a mermaid. We've all been through a lot, but you can't take the words of a toddler so seriously."

Brittany wished she could be so sure that Macy hadn't seen Serena and her crew splashing around, but even if the mermaids had somehow escaped, what could she do other than wait for them to show up again? Hopefully, they wouldn't bother. She couldn't fight them now that she might be pregnant. *For heaven's sake, I completely forgot about the pregnancy test!* She ran into the bathroom to retrieve the thin plastic strip and forced herself not to look at it alone. "Hey, everybody come here!" she yelled.

"I would never have thought I'd want to be in the room with my daughter while she held an object she'd peed on, but I'm so glad I'm here for this. Whatever the result is, we're here for you guys." Her dad choked on his words, but his eyes sparkled. Susan ran into the living room from the kitchen, wiping her brow with a tissue. No question about it, grandchildren born into this family would join Macy on the highest of pedestals. Luckily, there was plenty of love to go around.

All eyes on Brittany, she looked at Ryan. "Here we go." He nodded and smiled.

Staring at the test, Brittany's brain wouldn't allow her to interpret the symbol the lines made. After what seemed like an eternity, the result resonated. She held up the stick. "It's positive!" She finally understood the glow used to describe pregnant women. It came from within and radiated outward when a mother realizes she is helping grow something beautiful with so much potential to impact and influence the world. No wonder mothers became so upset when their children disappointed them. With the bonding experience that began in the womb and continued throughout the child's life, mothers felt like a piece of them had gone astray, never to be reclaimed again. Of course, they never stopped believing in their children, regardless of what they did.

Processing her emotions and thoughts, Brittany had been oblivious to everyone else's response. Ryan signed, "I love you," pulling her in for a hug. Behind him, her mom signed, "Proud," wiping a tear from her eye, and her dad smiled before pretending to have something in his eye, even though everyone knew he was crying.

When Ryan let go, Blake and Elaina ran toward her for a group hug. Pulling away, they both expressed their happiness. "Thanks, sisters. I don't have the first clue about being a mom. I'm probably the last person who should take this journey."

Blake furrowed her brow. "That's not true. You are an awesome aunt to Macy." Brittany's nerves tingled as she reflected on the events of the past few days. She hoped her sister was right.

"Even though Maggie kidnapped her under my watch?" Brittany asked, fidgeting with her thumb.

"I'm sorry that I blamed you when it happened, and I have to live with that mistake." Blake's hands trembled as she signed. "I hope you'll forgive me for being such a jerk when it happened." Blake hung her head, staring at the ground.

"You know I already have." Brittany patted her hand. "Anyway, look on the bright side—Parker and Maggie can't ever come back; thank God! But I still feel a little uneasy about the mermaids' whereabouts. I wish I could dive to check on them, but I just don't feel comfortable *now*."

"I agree. You definitely shouldn't go. I'll send Granny and Nancy to check it out after the wedding. That's the safest option, especially since you're pregnant!" Blake patted her belly. "Speaking of which, you're eating for two now, a great excuse not to hold back while having dinner. I wonder what excuse I can use to eat an extra helping of shrimp and cobbler…"

Brittany laughed but looked over at Ryan, who smiled. Her life was about to change in so many ways. She pictured living in the Lowcountry, a rambling old house with a wraparound porch, a loving and supportive husband, two darling kids and a dog, and hopefully, no ghosts other than Granny Mason and Nancy. No one had it all, but she and Ryan were about to come pretty damn close to having a perfect life.

Was she ready for this? *Yes! Tomorrow, I'll be someone's wife, and in less than a year, I'll be someone's Mom!* The rest of the evening, Brittany allowed herself to daydream about the future. Her pregnancy might not have happened in her time frame, but her heart was full all the same. *Forever starts tomorrow.*

Other books by Stephanie Edwards

Pearls of Wisdom: An adult coloring book
Did you love Nancy Parsons' colloquialisms? Get better acquainted with her sass in Pearls of Wisdom, an adult coloring book full of Southern charm.

The Haunting on Palm Court: Book 1
Blake Nelson flees her abusive, cheating fiance for her grandmother's beach cottage. He follows her there and tries to murder her. In a twist of events, he dies in an accident. His malevolent spirit returns to torment her, and the haunting intensifies when she reconnects with an old flame.

Coming in 2021 — Christmas on Palm Court: Book 3
Elaina Nelson has the perfect life—success in her career, a fiancé she adores and a supportive family. When Elaina least expects it, she uncovers a gift that sets her apart from her sisters. Will this blessing be her undoing?

Visit stephedwardswrites.com for purchasing details and information on Stephanie Edwards' upcoming books.

Made in the USA
Las Vegas, NV
07 May 2021